PERFECT SILENCE

Letters from the Past

TINA CLOUGH

PERFECT SILENCE

Copyright © Tina Clough 2023

The author asserts her moral right to be identified as the author of this work.

PAPERBACK ISBN 978-1-99-118717-8

A catalogue record of this book is available from the National Library of New Zealand

Lightpool Publishing

www.lightpoolpublishing.com

Cover and book design by Andrene Low

Prologue

Saskia Ormond could not remember the last time she had screamed at anyone or even raised her voice in anger; it just wasn't the kind of thing she did. From the time she was a tiny tot her father had reasoned and explained, trained her to moderate her reactions and it was only in retrospect she realised how unusual he must have been. For a single father to bring up a baby from new-born and study full-time would be a hard task for anyone, but when she considered his age at the time she now found it incredible that he had been so patient.

There must have been occasions when her grandmother had stepped in, but in the main her twenty-year-old father had taken charge of his the three-weeks-old daughter and created a tiny, independent family. Saskia had adopted her father's characteristics of being self-contained and quietly assured and had early developed the habit of making her own decisions and keeping herself occupied. Later these qualities had given her a certain aura of aloofness and made her desirable as a friend to be acquired when she got to high school, at the age when most girls worried about fitting in. But behind the public façade of quiet self-possession was an impulsive and joyful personality, and as time went on she learnt to make ad-hoc decisions about which persona to present in different situations.

But just then, blazing with fury and indignation, she screamed at her lover to 'get out *now* and never let me set eyes on you again'. Her anger was partly directed at herself for being so unobservant that she hadn't picked up on the little signs that he had another life and was just using her.

She shut the door behind him and remained standing in the hall, breathing hard and lost in a welter of conflicting emotions, but the feeling at the top of the list was a sense of betrayal. He had deceived and used her, but she had failed to see it, she had trusted him and confided in him, while he had consistently and cleverly lied from the very beginning.

Strangely, she was suddenly quite calm and even had a fleeting thought that nearly made her laugh. 'What a great scene this would be in a book,' she said out loud. 'It would have been better if I'd chucked him out naked and tossed his clothes after him, of course, but it's too late for that now.'

She gave a little choke of laughter and thought, isn't it odd, I'm not crying, because I'm not sad, I'm just very, very angry. At myself and at him, but mostly at him. "I might put you in a book, you lying bastard,' she said out loud.

Chapter 1

Saskia always looked forward to her father's visit the two first weeks in February. He came over from Sydney at the same time every year, a routine he had formed about ten years earlier.

'It fits perfectly,' Ross had explained on that first occasion when he had given her no choice about getting together over Christmas. 'By the end of January, I'll have been on the dig at up in the Northern Territory for nearly six weeks, Oenpelli again, and I'll have exactly two weeks until my classes start. It's the perfect gap.'

'But what about grandpa and Christmas?' she had asked. But Ross had it all planned, as usual. He would fly to Sydney to have three days with his father and his brother's family and then return to Oenpelli to continue working on the dig.

'Don't worry,' he had said. 'You do whatever you

want, come over for those couple of day too, if you want to, maybe stay a bit longer - or leave it to next year. We'll have our two weeks to ourselves in February this year. Or you could go to Canada and have a white Christmas with Robert and Claudia.'

Ross's second brother had lived in Canada with his Canadian wife for twenty or more years, so Saskia's relatives were thin on the ground in New Zealand. Her usual mid-year trip to stay with Ross in Sydney for a fortnight had been enjoyable in the quiet way it always was, but lately she had often wished that they lived in the same country. Maybe it was getting older, she thought, that fortieth birthday creeping ever closer and things that seemed insignificant ten years ago took on a level of importance she would never have expected when she was younger.

Of course, she didn't mind when Ross came, because she worked from home and could easily organise her life around him at any time of the year. Sometimes she told a friend about life as an only child with Ross as a solo father, usually in connection with him coming for a visit and someone asking about him before or after meeting him. A few of her friends had met him many times, and Marian thought he was the most interesting father anyone could have. Lizzie, who had met him twice during his last visit, had made no comment afterwards, but she had been very interested to hear Saskia's story.

'It's hard to imagine for someone like me, who

grew up in a family of six children,' she had said when Saskia had told her about her childhood with Ross. 'Our house was always full of visiting kids, and people coming to stay and sleeping on the floor or big birthday parties – and, of course, *never* tidy. I doubt if there was ever more than five minutes when every surface in the kitchen was clear of cups or dirty dishes or sticky butter knives left by someone who rushed in to grab a jam sandwich.'

Saskia had laughed at this picture of domestic chaos and said, 'And I can't imagine what that would be like. We had such a routine, Ross and I – we had to, I can see that now when I look back. For a guy at just turning twenty-one to study full-time or nearly full-time and bring up a tiny baby, who grew into a toddler! I don't know how he coped, and if he hadn't been so organised we would have foundered.'

When Ross visited her these days they sat in perfect, companiable silence on opposite sides of her dining table after breakfast with second cups of coffee beside them, both with their laptops and on his side papers strewn singly and in untidy piles. After a couple of hours, he would look up and say, 'I could do with a long walk now. Coming?'

Practically the same words every morning, followed by coffee or lunch at different locations every day. Just like everything they did in her childhood with routines for every task. It was probably the only way he had been able to keep track of everything, his studies, her school activities, food, laundry; everything was on his shoulders. Being a solo father and student required self-discipline, so every Monday night, straight after dinner, they would empty the wastepaper basket and the kitchen rubbish, put it in the bin and take it to the sidewalk for early morning collection. They got up at twenty to seven and made her school lunch, and had the same breakfast every morning, before she was dropped at school on the dot of eight when the school grounds were open for the early children. They read a story before bed, and every year on her birthday her bedtime was set to fifteen minutes later. When she turned ten and Ross was a lecturer at the university he said she could go to bed whenever she liked, so long as she didn't do anything noisy while he was working. They hardly ever watched TV, never played any boardgame except Scrabble, and never left the city to go on holiday, and they only left the city to go on digs or to visit relatives. Sometimes Ross went on a dig alone, if it was in a remote and inhospitable place and Saskia went to stay with her grandparents, Ross's parents.

Friends who got to hear this story from a straight-faced Saskia were inclined to express pity or sympathy, assuming she had felt deprived, and she would laugh and say, 'I *loved* it. Ross taught me to be self-reliant and to keep busy, and I was never bored. I had to use my imagination and keep myself motivated. When I realised other children went to swimming classes I asked if I could go too, and he organised it with another parent. When I wanted to learn to knit, he asked my grandmother to teach me next time I stayed. When I wanted a computer he bought me one. When I wanted a bike he taught me to ride it and taught me the road rules. I always had everything I needed or wanted. So, OK – maybe he wasn't great with hugs and kisses, but I knew he loved me, and he would have supported any ambition of mine however outlandish. If I'd said I had my heart set on being a trapeze artist, he would have sorted out a place for me to go and learn.'

She had never told anyone, not one single person, how Ross became a solo parent just before he turned twenty-one. She avoided questions about what happened to her mother, not because it was too painful, but because she understood, from when she first learnt the precise details about it at age fifteen, that the story would be too interesting and unusual not to be repeated and spread, probably widely, and to her it was private. Her father taught her how to look at it in a way that made her understand why her mother left her, how to accept it and not resent it.

'This is how it was,' he said when she asked at the age of six. 'I did tell you that some people have a mum, and some don't. Well, everyone has one to start with of course – no mums, no babies. Your mum left you with me because I wanted you, I really did, and her job meant she couldn't take you with her. So, she went away and then she never came back.'

'What was she called? Was she pretty?' asked six-year-old Saskia and her father said, 'She was very pretty and her name was Amanda.' And that was the end of the conversation at that time.

When Saskia was eleven she asked what her mother did and where she was now, because she had seen her birth certificate when they got it out, so she could have her own passport instead of being on Ross's. She had seen that her mother's surname name was Williams and that she was an American citizen. Her father told her he didn't know anything about her life now, and Saskia said, 'OK, I just wanted to know if she did get famous in some important job.'

And Ross replied that Amanda had all the makings of someone who was bound to get famous in some important job, so she had probably done that, and he could find out if she wanted to know.

When Saskia was fifteen she thought of asking again, but she didn't find the right moment. As she got older, she had wondered if he never mentioned it again because it was too painful, so that summer holiday, which she spent with her grandparents while Ross was on a dig, she asked her grandmother what she knew.

'Nothing, darling,' said her grandmother. 'We know absolutely nothing, we never did! Your dad was twenty when this happened – the pregnancy, I mean, first year at university. He came home and told us he was having a baby, that's how he put it, and he was going to keep it. The mother – I mean, your mother – was leaving you behind and returning overseas as soon as you were born, back to wherever she came from, which we also never found out.'

'Harsh!' said teenaged Saskia. 'What a selfish girl!'

'Unusual,' said her grandmother. 'Ross said at the time that she was very unusual, and determined and serious. Enormously ambitious. You should ask him sometime – you're old enough now and you know he'd never lie to you. Does it bother you that she went away and left you behind? Don't forget we all love you.'

'Oh, no,' said Saskia. 'I'm not neurotic about it or anything, I just wonder what became of her.'

'So, this is how it was,' continued her grandmother. 'Once you were born and he had taken possession of you, so to speak, he turned up here with you in a sling on his chest - he used to have you in that sling when he studied or did the housework. He said hearing his heartbeat was good for you. You were three weeks old the first time we saw you and he said, "meet your granddaughter, she's called Saskia". And he never for a moment considered that he might ask us to bring you up. We did offer, and he just looked at us as if we were mad!' Her grandmother shook her head and laughed at the memory. 'It was quite funny, we laughed about it afterwards, your granddad and I.

Ross said, "God no, she's my daughter and I'll bring her up myself" and that was that.'

And Saskia, to her grandmother's surprise, felt no urge to find her mother and she still didn't. She had tried to explain it to her grandmother, saying seriously, 'She couldn't be bothered with me, because she was probably too ambitious, but dad really wanted me. I mean how many guys would want to bring up a baby at twenty-one? And perhaps you *can* miss someone you never knew, perhaps I'm unusual, but I don't feel I have to start searching for her, I never did.'

Chapter 2

The invitation from her publisher to attend a cocktail party to celebrate the fiftieth anniversary of the company's first book took Saskia by surprise because she hadn't realised it was only created in the 1970's. Not that she had ever considered it, but if anyone had asked she would have said it was probably a hundred years old.

An hour after reading the email she was still pondering how important the celebration was, and if she had to go. 'Fifty!' she said as she took the loaf of banana bread out of the tin she had baked it in and put it on a rack to cool, ready to take to Marian's the next day. 'Do companies really have parties for half-centuries?'

But she did decide to go, if only to check out the other authors. She rarely went to her publishers' Christmas Party because at that time of the year it usually clashed with something put on by one of her friends, and she'd rather go to their parties. Being part of the corporate pre-Christmas merry-go-round had never been part of her list of important things to do, and she only ever attended things when her editor told her she had to.

On a glorious spring evening a couple of weeks later, and slightly reluctantly, Saskia arrived in O'Connell Street, took the lift to level six and was met by a cacophony of voices when the lift doors slid open. The party was in full swing and had spilt over onto the landing, with music, voices and occasional shrieks of laughter escaping from further inside the office.

Saskia wound her way between groups, ducked to avoid a short waiter with a tray of glasses held not quite high enough to be safe, and found the office crammed with people and noise including a superfluous and very amplified guitar player singing something nobody could make out. In the far corner of the large reception area, she spotted her editor in the corner beside the huge potted cordyline she had always admired. Deciding that making sure she was noted as being present was a good idea, considering how many times she had made excuses not to come, she made her way through the crowd.

'I'm so glad you could come!' said Audrey and air-kissed Saskia's cheek, leaving the words "this time" suspended in the air between them like a little unspoken reproach. 'You must meet Bruno – Bruno, this is our lovely Saskia Ormond, I'm sure you know her work.'

'Of course, I know who you are, very pleased to meet you.' He smiled and Saskia smiled back, and wondered if he would ask if she was writing something at the moment, which was the most common thing people said when they first met her and either recognised her name or were told she was an author.

'It's an impossible thing to reply to,' Saskia had said to Marian once after a party where she had been asked this three times. 'The only reasonable answer it "yes" and then both you and the person who asked are stuck, because what else could I add and what else could they say? It drives me nuts! I wish people would just take for granted that I'm always writing something and not ask.'

And Marian had said, in her usual calm and reasonable way, 'You could say "no, I'm taking a break" and then change the subject.'

Then Audrey spotted someone else she needed to greet and said quickly, 'I'll have to leave you two for a moment, sorry!' and disappeared through the crowd, and Bruno turned to Saskia and said, 'And that doesn't mean she'll be back in a moment, of course. We'll probably not see her again tonight.'

It made her laugh, how cool he sounded and he

infectious his smile was. 'Never mind her, tell me what your link to this bedlam is – why you're here.'

'God knows,' he said modestly, as if he was genuinely puzzled. 'I have no idea, but I thought it sounded like an interesting crowd to meet, maybe job opportunities.'

Ten minutes later they were still in the corner with the potted cordyline, safely out of the churn of people slowly revolving around the space. Their glasses were empty, the food trays had passed them by and Bruno, who could see a lot further than Saskia, said, 'No food or drink coming our way just now. How about we leave this madhouse and go for a quiet drink and something to eat somewhere we can hear ourselves talk?'

'This is conveniently close. I've never been here before,' said Saskia at Le Chef and looked around the brick and wood interior. 'It's very cosy, is it one of your favourites?'

'Only since I've lived in the city,' said Bruno and waited until a waiter had delivered their glasses of wine before he continued. 'I'm in the process of leaving my wife and I've got a little flat just around the corner, just for now, until everything's sorted out.'

What a strange way of putting it, thought Saskia and took a sip of her wine and wondered if "in the process of leaving" meant that he had moved out, but was not officially separated? Or had he moved out and was separated, but not yet divorced? Aloud she said, 'I've never been married. Do you have children?'

'No children,' he said and looked as if he was pleased at this lack of complications. 'We were one of those selfish couples who always put off having children – too busy, too intent on earning money and paying off the mortgage. You know the kind of thing. And then it dawned on us that we'd grown apart and had little in common, so we decided to split.'

'So, what kind of job opportunity were you hoping for when you went to that cocktail party?' asked Saskia when they had decided to order dinner and stay where they were. 'Do you want to get into editing?'

'I've been doing some PR writing, press releases and stuff on the side for a while -nothing much, but I enjoy it. And you never know who you'll meet at that kind of party, so I took the chance and went.'

His smile was a nice mixture of cheeky and confiding, and made Saskia feel he had opened up to her in a way he might not have with someone else, as if he trusted her to accept his honesty and not judge him harshly.

'It's hard to change what you're doing at my age – no history of similar work to fall back on, or not enough anyway. But tell me about your work. I know what you do obviously, but where do you write?'

She looked thoughtfully at him and wondered

what he could possibly mean. Did he think she wrote at the publisher's office, or maybe that she had a little office somewhere in town, where she went at nine every morning?

'I write at home,' she replied without emphasis and waited to see what his response would be, and he grinned. 'Of course, you write at home. I mean, do you have a study with a gorgeous old rosewood desk and a lovely old painting hanging over it for you to look at while you think of ways to kill people?'

Saskia burst out laughing at how much more amusing he was than she had appreciated at the start, when she had mainly noticed his smile and how good looking he was.

'No, I'm sad to confess I don't. I write at a modern little height-adjustable desk in my living room where I can look out at the view while I think of ways to kill people. And before you ask, no, I don't have set hours to write either, I do it in bits and pieces and sometimes I write for hours at a stretch because I know exactly where the story is going.'

At the end of the evening Bruno offered to take her home, but she turned him down. 'Oh no, there's no need,' she said lightly, knowing from past experience how many men liked to try their luck at her front door. 'If you live just around the corner you certainly don't want to traipse around town just to see me home,' she said briskly. 'I'll take a taxi like I always do.'

She got her phone out as she spoke and pressed the fast dial for the taxi company she always used. Intrigued and interested she might be, but not to the point of letting him into her flat at half past eleven after a first date. She would stick to her usual habits, she thought in the taxi ten minutes later, after agreeing with Bruno that they must meet again and sharing phone numbers. She would continue to pay for herself and wait to get to know him better before taking the next step, as she had done from the time she first started getting well-known as a writer. The world was full of pitfalls and being even moderately well-known had sometimes proved a drawback when it came to men, particularly men who had writing ambitions of their own. Few realised that her lifestyle, and that fact that she didn't need a part-time job to support herself, was not due to book sales, but to the sale of film and TV rights; being commercially viable, as Audrey put it, at what point Saskia always told her she'd prefer to be commercially desirable, rather than viable.

When she stood in her bathroom tying her hair back before going to bed, she thought she must ask Bruno what kind of PR material he wrote, because they'd got side-tracked and she never found out. Maybe for a travel agency, she thought, I could picture him in the travel business. And then she laughed at herself for being silly, turned the bathroom light off and went to bed.

Chapter 3

It wasn't until her fourth date with Bruno that she got around to asking where he worked. 'I was going to ask you,' she said over dinner one night. 'But you're so entertaining that I keep forgetting.'

'Mason and Williams Limited,' said Bruno. 'And it's dead boring, I just write a lot of PR material and sales pitches and sometimes a little blog type thing for the website. But tell me more about your dad – you started and then we ordered and never went back to him. What kind of dig is it he goes to every summer holiday?'

Saskia told him about the Oenpelli dig and the kind of things they had found there. 'I went once,' she said and made a face at the memory. 'I barely survived. It's always over 30 degrees, and I mean *always* and often a lot more, then add in a river called Alligator River - the name tells you everything you need to know - and exposed hills of red rock like crouching dinosaurs and *dust*. A lot of dust. The kind of environment that seems like hell on earth to me, and definitely not for anyone who wants variety, a cool breeze, or who gets red eyes from dust.'

Bruno laughed. 'At the risk of sounding like a wimp of a man, I have to confess I agree with you. Not that I mind the outdoors, but there's got to be some degree of civilisation nearby, a comfortable hotel and restaurants with air conditioning. But I did once go to Cairns and then north to Daintree and did the rainforest canopy walk which was amazing, a real experience. We should do it together some time!'

'I'd like that,' said Saskia. 'I thought about it once a couple of years ago and I asked my friend Lizzie to come. I'd just got to know her then, and she said she was keen to go out to the Great Barrier reef too, but then she had to have knee surgery and we never got around to reorganising it.'

'Gloom and doom - soon it's time for the annual duty visit,' said Bruno over dessert. 'I usually manage to avoid visiting the parents during the year, but at Christmas I mostly don't have a choice.'

Saskia poked her spoon through the burnt sugar top of her crème caramel and thought how luscious and inviting that sound was, an audible foretaste of the creamy deliciousness underneath. 'Where do they live?'

'Invercargill – nearly as far away as you can get,

which is a blessing. Not that I mind going down there, but I promised to spend nearly three weeks this year. It's my dad's seventy-fifth birthday just after New Year's and the whole extended family are gathering from all over.'

'Why do you say you *manage* to avoid visits? Don't you get on with them?'

Bruno looked as if the question surprised him. 'Oh well, you know how it is. You spend a lot of time sitting around talking about nothing much and there will be kids everywhere, teenagers skulking in corners glued to their phones. And endless sessions of reminiscing and arguing about who it was who caused the Christmas tree to topple thirty years ago. Not my scene, really.'

Saskia changed the subject with a feeling of surprised disappointment. It seemed so far removed from how she felt about her own father and grandparents that it was hard to understand. Was it just that he didn't fit in with his family or was he selfish? Did he only enjoy things on his terms? That tone of near resentment when he described their family getting together had sounded callous and uncaring, and she wondered if the charm and the fun conversations they usually had concealed another side of Bruno, one that was not so appealing.

'I love my dad,' she said now. 'I really do, he's not just my father, he's my friend just as much as he is my father, and we talk about everything.'

'Lucky you!' said Bruno flippantly and then his phone buzzed quietly. He got it out, looked at the screen and put it back in his pocket.

'Do you want to take that?' asked Saskia. 'I don't mind if you do.'

'No, just someone sending a text about getting together. Which I'll turn down because I don't much like them, I'll make an excuse.'

Much later that evening, when she closed the door behind Bruno, she thought back to the conversation in the restaurant and wondered if she was making too much out of a casual conversation. Perhaps she was being judgmental, and comparing Bruno's relationship with his parents to her own close bond with Ross might be unfair. She knew others who had less than close ties to their families and probably avoided seeing them too often, though few would be as open about it as Bruno was.

A couple of weeks before Christmas, when Bruno had spent the whole night at Saskia's flat for the first time, Matthew called while they were having breakfast. Saskia glanced at her phone and said, 'Sorry, I have to take this.'

She got up from her stool at the breakfast bar and walked across to the living room end and sat down to talk to him, and as usual the conversation provided a couple of opportunities for her to tease him.

'Who was the guy you left with from that cocktail party the other week?' asked Matthew. 'I've never seen him before – is he an author?'

'Who was it *you* left with?' asked Saskia instead of replying.

'Don't be silly, I didn't leave with anyone, and you wouldn't have seen me leave anyway. You were leaving just as I arrived, and you didn't even notice me. Is he your new date?'

'Just a new friend,' she said casually, but laughing inside. 'Nobody you need to get jealous of, Matthew.'

'Of course, I'm not jealous, but I was intrigued because Audrey asked me if I knew anything about him. She said she'd introduced you to him, but she'd only just met him herself and she didn't even know his surname, hadn't seen him before.'

'Probably a gate crasher,' said Saskia. 'I'll ask him next time I see him. And you'll be pleased to hear that the book is coming along nicely now. I've got past that horrid early stage when nothing sounds right, when trying to get the story to go where you want it to go is all effort and no pleasure. It's progressing nicely, well on the way to meet the deadline if I keep up the current pace.'

When they ended the call and Saskia sat down to finish her breakfast she noticed the strange look Bruno gave her. He's put two and two together, she thought, he's figured out that we were talking about him, but as yet he doesn't know what Matthew just told me.

'Did you gate-crash that cocktail party?' she asked, looking straight at him. 'My agent just asked me who you are. My editor told him she only knew your fist name and had no idea why you were there.' She kept her eyes on his, not wanting to miss his reaction.

But Bruno didn't seem in the least flustered or embarrassed, he smiled and said, 'Yeah, I did. I heard about it from someone I know, and I thought it might be a chance to get known to a few people who might be useful. Just an opportunistic impulse, not what I normally do.' He reached over and put his hand on hers. 'Little did I know that I'd meet the most important person in my life there. Not at all what I expected.'

'Very enterprising,' she replied lightly, though gate-crashing a fairly formal by-invitation-only cocktail party wasn't something she felt comfortable with. But Bruno was a very different person from her; he had other life rules and went his own way, so when he left for work she put it out of her mind and turned her laptop on to do some writing before she tidied up.

Chapter 4

Saskia always looked forward to parties at Marian and Tony's because they never had adults-only parties. Over the years she had got to know a wide variety of children of all ages at their place, a couple of times the parents of a guest, and once an ancient grandfather, who spent the evening reading in the highbacked armchair in the corner of their living room with his hearing aid turned off.

'You're so unusual,' said Saskia when she and Marian were preparing cocktail food for the pre-Christmas party. 'I don't know anyone else who has the kind of parties you do - you even have people's kids come to sit-down dinner parties.'

'What's not to understand?' Marian wrenched to top of a cylinder of toothpicks which erupted out and flew all over the bench.

'Oh damn! But it's nice to include people's kids

and setting up a separate table for them is no trouble.' And then she laughed a little and added, 'And I've noticed that the parents who bring their kids always behave better than they do at other people's places when the kids aren't with them. Parents and children monitor each other's behaviour, isn't it funny?'

'It reminds me of your birthday parties when we were at primary school,' said Saskia from where she was crouching and picking up toothpicks from the floor. 'Your mum always invited whole families, I used to love it.'

She got to her feet with a dozen toothpicks in her hand. 'Where do you want these?'

'Just put them here,' said Marian and pointed. 'They're too thin to pick up germs and we'll need them for the little meatballs in a minute.'

'Really, is that a scientific fact? Too thin to pick up germs?' Saskia grinned and turned to peer into the oven where dozens of tiny meatballs were slowly turning crisp and brown.

'I'll tell you what my grandmother used to say before she lost the plot.' Marian turned to get a platter out and handed it to Saskia. 'We'll put the meatballs on this with the bowl of hot sauce in the centre, and a toothpick in each one and it's done. But yes, grandma used to say a little clean dirt never hurt anyone. And reading about causes of the increase in asthma I'm beginning to think she was right.'

The evening turned into a typical summer party

with people moving from inside to the terrace and back, younger children playing chasing games and teenagers clustered on the grass under a tree with lights strung through it.

'Look at them all with their damn phones like they've grown prosthetic hand attachments,' said Tony from behind Saskia where she sat on the edge of the terrace talking to Lizzie. 'And where did you meet Bruno? I had no idea you two knew each other.'

Saskia craned her neck and looked up at him. 'Would you mind sitting down so I don't get a crick in my neck – or come and stand in front of us? I'm too lazy to move. And where did *you* meet Bruno, anyway? I didn't know you knew him either.'

'He sold us this house six years ago,' said Tony and jumped down on to stand on the lawn beside them. 'I spotted you having dinner together when I went out for a drink with a client. I asked Marian if you were dating him, and she said she had no idea. You could have brought him, he's very entertaining - and a damn good real estate agent, very helpful.'

'We've been out a couple of times,' said Saskia evasively and for some reason she couldn't define she decided to make it sound casual. 'He's away this weekend, or I might have.'

Lizzie cast a slanting glance at Saskia, as if she was curious, but nothing more was said, and then a couple joined them and the conversation became general, but Saskia was aware of that glance in her direction once or twice more during the evening and thought she must soon tell Lizzie about Bruno.

Late that night Saskia looked up from the book she was reading in bed and wondered at herself, slightly confused by her own behaviour. Lizzie was her closest friend apart from Marian, so why hadn't she mentioned Bruno to either of them?

Having read in the morning paper that the holiday season drink-drive blitz started that day and lasted until after New Year, Saskia took a taxi to Lizzie's place two days before Christmas. Expensive, she thought as she waited to be picked up, but not as expensive as getting fined. Lizzie lived on the other side of the city centre, in a little townhouse on the very edge of the Remuera golf course. And why did she worry about the cost of a taxi anyway? Sometimes these strange little remnants from her early life with Ross, like the habit of looking carefully at the cost of everything, popped up and took her by surprise.

'Grange Road, Remuera, please,' she said to the driver. 'I can't remember the number, but I'll tell you where it is when we get there.'

'That's what they all say.' The woman laughed. 'Everyone knows which street, but nobody knows the number. Do you know why?'

'I have no idea - maybe we're swamped with too much random information these days.'

'We don't send birthday cards and Christmas cards or write letters like people used to. We never need to know the street number until we're in a taxi.'

Saskia considered thisand had to admit the driver was right. She hadn't sent a card for years. And if we'd never been to someone's place before we'd have to text them and ask, she thought, and realised she had just remembered Lizzie's number from when she sent her flowers for her birthday, but she didn't tell the driver, who was so pleased with her own theory that it seemed a pity to mention it now.

When Saskia arrived, Lizzie's front door was wide open, and she walked right through the living room and out into the garden where four women were sitting at a table loaded with edible treats and bottles of wine.

'Saskia, hi!' said Lizzie. 'I think you've met Lotta and Mandy before? Oh good, and this is Rita who's just started working at the library – Rita this is my friend Saskia. I'll go and close the front door now we're all here.'

'We've just been upstairs in Lizzie's bedroom to show Rita the view over the golf course,' said Lottie and laughed. 'It's the routine thing now since Lizzie moved here – everyone gets taken upstairs to see the gorgeous view. She should convert her bedroom to a sitting room.'

'No way!' said Lizzie back coming across the little garden. 'I love that I can only see it from my bedroom – it's such a nice thing to wake up to in the mornings and then I go downstairs, and I can't be seen by anyone. It was one of the reasons I bought this house - no neighbour on the golf course side.'

'You could garden in the nude,' said Rita.

'Oh, please! I don't want to even think about it.' Lizzie shuddered dramatically. 'Not a sight I want to expose in daylight.'

The dinner was delicious as it always was at Lizzie's, with several small dishes and lots of things on the side. 'You must spend hours cooking and preparing - it's like tasting menu in a restaurant,' said Mandy. 'I don't know how you do it, but it's wonderful.'

'I like cooking, and it's fun to do something a bit different – *and* it means everyone finds something they like.' She held out a dish of salmon pasta to Saskia. 'Try this, I think you've had it before. I've changed the sauce and I think it's an improvement. So, how serious is this thing with the real estate agent? What was his name?'

Here it comes, thought Saskia and quietly admired the tactical approach, because in front of these women she might not get away with being evasive, and why would she want to be evasive, anyway? She still didn't understand her slight reluctance to talk about Bruno.

'His name is Bruno Robinson' she said. 'And it's not serious, Lizzie, I've only seen him half a dozen times.'

'Tony said he's the best real estate agent ever.' Lizzie pushed a dish of Moroccan lamb across the table towards Mandy. 'Try this, I'm blending the spices myself now instead of buying them ready-mixed. Tell me what you think, you've been there, after all.'

Lottie got her phone out. 'What was his name again? I might recommend him to my brother. They're talking about putting their house on the market and someone who comes with a personal recommendation is always good. They were just saying the other day that they don't know anything about real estate agents – they've lived in that house for twenty years.'

'But he's not in real estate now,' said Saskia. 'He works for some downtown company writing press releases and stuff, sits in an office all day. It seems a waste in a way – he's very good-looking and fun, which must have helped when he was selling houses.'

'No, he's still selling houses,' said Lottie and held up her phone so Saskia could see it. 'Here he is on Facebook, a post that's dated a week ago about a house he's selling for someone in Glenn Innes – not far from here.'

'Maybe I got it wrong,' said Saskia and made an effort to sound casual. 'Maybe he's doing press releases and things for the real estate company. I can't say I was paying much attention at the time because I was reading a menu.' She noticed Lizzie's glance and ignored it. What a thin excuse, she thought, but I was taken by surprise, I normally do better than that.

She turned to Rita, hoping to change the subject away from Bruno. 'You're the first Rita I've ever met, it's a great name.'

Lizzie and the other three women looked at each other and laughed while Saskia looked at them in confusion. 'Don't worry, they're not mad,' said Rita. 'I've just started working at the library, but before that I was very briefly a parking warden – everyone over forty or so thinks it's hilarious.'

Now everyone was watching Saskia's face expectantly, and suddenly she got it and laughed too. 'Aha, Rita, Rita, meter maid, like that Beetles song. Oh God, that *is* funny! Did you mum love the Beetles?'

'No, she wasn't into music much, but she loved Rita Hayworth, the film star from way back. Of course, mum is too young to have seen her films when they were new, but she got interested in her through an article somewhere and started reading about her, and that was it. I got christened Rita.'

'I remember seeing her in a film with Fred Astaire at that cinema in Wellington that show classic films, really old ones. My grandmother took me when I was about seven or eight,' said Lottie. 'She was an amazing dancer and she had gorgeous legs – Rita Hayworth, I mean, not my granny, best legs ever.'

Rita put her knife and fork down, held up one hand and started counting on her fingers, 'She had one, two, three, four, five husbands and a few very public love affairs. Having been named after her I've read a bit about her too. Not that I can remember who all those husbands were, but it's an impressive record and one of them was an Arab prince.'

Lottie picked up her phone, searched for a minute and said, 'Orson Welles was one of her husbands, so there was fame on both sides in that marriage.' She scrolled down further. 'None of them lasted long, though. Must have been something about her.'

For the first time ever, Saskia had Christmas on her own, which she didn't really think about until Christmas Eve when the courier delivered a box with three presents from Australia, just in time. One each from her father, grandfather, and her uncle's family. She straight away sent an email to all of them to say the parcel had arrived, promised she wouldn't open the presents until the next morning and wished them all Merry Christmas. Then she looked around her flat, where she had no decorations, just the presents that had just been delivered and one from Lizzie and Marian respectively, all in a pile on her coffee table.

This was a first, and she tried to work out how she

felt about it. She usually either flew to Sydney to have a family Christmas with her father and the rest of the Ormonds, or she spent Christmas Day with Marian's family. This year the Australian Ormonds were in Fiji for two weeks, so her father was staying at the dig at Oenpelli, and Marian's clan had gone to her sister's place in Hawke's Bay. Lizzie, who had no family in New Zealand, would have been the perfect companion, but she had booked herself into a luxury lodge outside Taupo for five days for what she called her annual self-indulgence event, and there was nobody else Saskia particularly wanted to spend time with.

The afternoon seemed like any other day; she wrote for a while, made a cup of coffee and sat down to read, and thought how odd it was to be so calm with nothing to organise or prepare for and nowhere to go. She imagined other households where frantic preparations were underway, guest room beds being made and fridges full of food. On the whole, she didn't feel left out or deprived of something significant, it just felt any other day.

———————

Chapter 5

———————

Saskia had no idea when exactly Bruno would be back from the South Island visit to his family. He had texted her every couple of days, complaining about boredom, mediocre food, and tedious family routines, but he had said nothing about his return date, but now it was more than three weeks since he had left, and Saskia expected to hear from him any day. Not that she was exactly longing for him, but with so many of her friends away on holiday, lunch dates and invitations were thin on the ground.

On a Wednesday morning, when she was standing at the kitchen bench waiting for the water to boil for a cup of tea, her phone let out the new ring tone she had downloaded the other day so she could more easily decide if it was an incoming text or call. She raced to find the phone she had left on the bedside table again, which to some extent proved how useful the new ring tone was going to in avoiding voice messages or missed calls.

'Hello, my treasure, how are you?' said Bruno cheerfully. 'I'm back in the civilised world again and I can't wait to see you. How about dinner tonight?'

For some reason she didn't immediately understand, Saskia made a snap decision to pretend she was busy and said, 'Welcome back - nice to hear your voice again! I'm busy tonight, but I'm free tomorrow.'

'Busy on a Wednesday?' said Bruno and she heard the slight rancour in his voice and thought she knew why. Aloud she replied calmly, 'Yes, a Wednesday online meeting with people who haven't been able to coordinate themselves during office hours. Let's go out tomorrow night.'

When they ended the call she made the cup of tea and went back to her desk, deep in thought. Why had she said she was busy tonight? Was it because she didn't want him to think she had been sitting around waiting for him to come back with nothing to do while he was away? And had that same feeling been behind his slightly sulky question? The more she thought of it, the more likely it seemed. In the time they had been dating, right up until he left to visit his parents, she had nearly always been able to say yes to his suggestions about dinner or drinks, mostly just by chance, not because she didn't get other invitations. Maybe he thought he was her only source of entertainment, though she was certain she had mentioned seeing other friends and being invited out. It wasn't that she wanted to thwart him or put him in his place, more that she resented being taken for granted. She would take care tomorrow to not reveal her thoughts or it might create a lasting problem. The idea that he was one to harbour resentment wasn't new. There had been an earlier occasion when he had taken her by surprise with his reaction to something she said, but until now she hadn't thought about it again.

He was fun to be with, very entertaining and very handsome, which shouldn't have influenced any decisions of hers, it was just a added-value component. Even when he wasn't entertaining, he was what Marian and she used to call eye-candy when they were at high school. But in the back of her head a voice of warning reminded her of what she had found out at Lizzie's place just before Christmas, and she made a mental note to ask Bruno directly what his job was. Not that there was anything wrong with selling real estate, but lying about it was, and she would rather know for sure if he had deliberately deceived her.

Dinner the following evening was pleasant and intermittently hilarious as Bruno expanded on the boredom of his Christmas holiday, his lonely rambles to avoid the repetitive conversations and how dreadful the menu was at his parents' favourite restaurant where they had eaten twice. But by the time they were checking the dessert menu, Saskia had become uncomfortable with the ridicule and said abruptly, 'There must surely have been some nice moments, too, Bruno, it can't all have been boring or dreadful. You must have enjoyed meeting up with the wider family and seeing how their children have grown, all those simply, nice things.'

'Nope, I didn't!' said Bruno and smiled his wicked, charming smile. 'I found the whole thing exhausting and tedious. If it hadn't been my dad's seventy-fifth I wouldn't have gone. Not a single person had anything to say that was original, interesting or even controversial enough to start a debate. They all agree on everything – the even have this weird shorthand to remind each other of something they talked about last time they got together.'

"They got together", she noted wryly, not "we got together", so he saw himself as an outsider, someone who legally belonged to the family but had no emotional connection. It was a foreign concept for Saskia, who had grown up with a close bond with not only her father, but also with her uncles and her grandparents. And that kind of bond is important, she thought, as she listened with half an ear to Bruno telling her a story about the man he sat next to on the flight back. It's the emotional familial connections that define who we are and how we relate to other people.

How strange to be a person without those connections.

She was just about to tell him about some of the things she had done while he was away, when he surprised her by asking how the Zoom meeting had gone, so she had to invent a suitable story on the spot.

'Oh, fine,' she said vaguely. 'It was just about the plans and all that for the book I've nearly finished now. You know, there's got a be a blurb for the back cover, which I don't have any say in, of course, but I always try to push a bit if I think what they've come up with isn't good enough, and the same thing with the media release. It happens every time and though it's a formality from their point of view to include me in the discussion, they'll mostly do what they want whatever I say, but we still go through this process each time.'

Bruno's eyes lit up and he leaned forward across the table, the most intent she had ever seen him. 'Would you like me to come up with something you could present to them – a suggested blurb, I mean?'

Saskia remembered his reason for gate crashing the publisher's cocktail party and her resolution to ask him about his job and said, 'No, thanks, I've already done that. I think I write very good blurbs for my own books, not that they ever use them. Oh, wait – they did once a few years ago. But it reminds me, I never found out what it is you write for your company. Is it anything like blurbs, sales material?'

'Lots of it,' he said and grinned. 'The real estate company I work for pride themselves on catchy and clever advertising, and I'm very good at it, so I get used a lot.'

'Used a lot?' Saskia wasn't sure what he meant. 'Do they have others writing them too?'

'We all write out own, but I often get asked to improve those others have written. There's a trick to it, you see. You only have so many lines that will show under the photo people see first, so you've got to find a snappy way to entice people to open the whole post, look at the next dozen photos and maybe read the whole text.'

'Like e-book blurbs on Amazon,' said Saskia. 'Exactly the same. So, you sell houses, as well as write about them?'

'Of course,' he said on a surprised note. 'Surely you knew that?'

'I must have missed the vital link somehow.' Reassured now, Saskia laughed at herself and her suspicions. 'I thought you just wrote stuff, and I missed the important bit. Are you successful?'

'Very!' said Bruno, making no pretence at modesty. 'There's another knack you need when you sell properties, and that's the ability to grasp exactly what people think they can afford, and then show them things you know they'll really like – more expensive things. But not too expensive, just enough to make them feel they might be able to stretch to a slightly bigger mortgage and still manage. You tell them something about the more expensive house that appeals to their self-image and vanity, as if you understand how discerning they are, and that you know they'll appreciate these finer points. Flattery, really, but it often works.'

'But why? Is it like at MacDonalds when they ask if you want chips as well? Upselling? And if it is, what's the point?'

'More commission,' said Bruno matter-of-factly. 'The higher the price of the property, the more commission I get. And I'm a master of the art, even if I say it myself.'

Later that evening, when Saskia had made a heavy period with cramps the excuse for not having Bruno stay the night at her place, she lay awake for a long time trying to reconcile all the conflicting things she now had stored in her head. Some of them might be based on mistaken impressions, she thought, like the misunderstanding about what his job was, though she had a distinct memory of him saying he worked for a two-name company maybewith "limited" on the end, not a real estate firm's name, and no mention had been made of real estate. She wondered if he had made a snap decision tonight to be honest because he remembered some reaction of hers when she asked if he had gate-crashed that party. Other things that worried her were based on his inherent selfishness, and the way he talked so dismissively and unfeeling about his family and sometimes about other people. Perhaps she should just end it because any kind of long-term or serious involvement was unlikely. There had been some slightly uncomfortable moments right from the start, and perhaps good sex and fun dates didn't make it worthwhile to invest more time in someone who probably wouldn't last, however entertaining he was. Bruno had hinted a couple of times that he would love for them to live together, but this idea had not resonated with Saskia, who had no intention of ever sharing her daily life with anyone. Somehow she had understood, whether it had been implied or not, that he meant he should move in with her, which was not an option. She wanted to be able write when she felt like it, have peace and silence around her and decide for herself what she ate or when she went to bed. The trip to Thailand they were planning to take, which she had at first thought might be a good test of how they would function when they were in each other's company all day, every day for a fortnight, now got reclassified to 'just a trip' in her mind.

Chapter 6

Saskia couldn't remember the last time she had screamed at anyone or even raised her voice in anger; it just wasn't the kind of thing she did. From the time she was a tiny tot her father had reasoned and explained, trained her to moderate her reactions and it was only in retrospect she realised how unusual he must have been. For a single father to bring up a baby from new-born and at the same time study full-time would be a hard task for anyone, but when she considered his age at the time she found it incredible that he had been so patient.

But just now, a couple of weeks after Bruno's return, and blazing with rage and indignation, she screamed at him to 'get out *now* and never let me set eyes on you again'. Her fury was partly directed at herself for being so unobservant that she hadn't picked up on the little signs that indicated he was just using her. When she shut the door behind him, she remained standing in the hall, breathing hard and lost in a welter of conflicting emotions, but the feeling at the top of the list was a sense of betrayal. He had deceived and used her, but she had failed to see it, she had trusted him and confided in him, but he had lied from the very beginning. The fact that she had already developed doubts about them having any kind of future, was a different matter; this was trickery and deliberate deception.

Strangely, she was suddenly quite calm and even had a fleeting thought that nearly made her laugh. '*What* a great scene this would be in a book,' she said out loud to herself. 'It would have been better still if I'd thrown him out naked and chucked his clothes after him, but it's too late now.' Then she gave a little choke of laughter and thought, isn't it odd, I'm not crying, because I'm not sad, I'm just very, very angry. At myself and at him, but mostly at him. 'I might put you in a book, you lying bastard,' she said out loud.

She poured a glass of wine and went to sit in a chair on the balcony, looking out over the Viaduct Basin, which seemed to be nearly deserted. And as she had done so often since she bought the apartment, she blessed the fact that the building had been soundproofed with special insulation. It had been one of the things that made her decide to abandon her lovely little house in Freeman's Bay and move. The promise of an environment where she could write in perfect silence, live high up and have a gorgeous view all at the same time had been irresistible. And tonight, she hoped the sound proofing had done its job and prevented the neighbours from hearing her screaming.

She sat there for an hour, alternating between reading and gazing out over the boats in the marina and further out, to the open harbour with occasional reflections on the night dark water. It was too late for the ferries heading across to Birkenhead or out to Waiheke Island, and the late January night was calm and warm, and very quiet. Over to her left the lights on the harbour bridge created an arc across the water and her gaze tracked the light of cars from the North Shore, up the slope and down on the city side. You would hardly know there was a big city not that far behind her. Traffic noise hardly ever reached her here; her block of flats faced the sea, and the nearest street was behind another block of flats that sat directly behind hers. I love this place, she thought. I never needed those three bedrooms in the house, I always wrote at my little desk in the living room there too. I've never felt the need to lock myself away in a special space to be creative, this apartment is perfect.

Before she went to bed she made some notes in one of her notebooks, some ideas about a new book where Bruno might become a fictional character, a deceiver and liar in a different context, perhaps a final crime novel, despite having made up her mind to stop writing them. She could make him a bit worse, make him a fraudster as well, or get him killed by a furious woman he had tricked, or maybe he would kill someone to silence them. She smiled to herself, added another couple of notes and realised she couldn't have been even slightly in love with Bruno, or she wouldn't be sitting here making notes about him as a fictional character. Maybe it was just lust on her side and the enjoyment of his sense of fun, which she had to admit he had in abundance. A very charming and entertaining man, so easy to be with, not to say too easy to be with. What it had been on his side was harder to figure out, but maybe he just liked having different women on the go at the same time. Perhaps it was a power trip or an ego trip, or maybe he was simply over-sexed.

But planning a plot configuration was irresistible, and she continued working on it when she went to bed. She could make him a serial cheater, a man who would come straight from sex with someone else, have a shower and get into bed with his lover – like the real Bruno. The ultimate cheater, she thought, a man who not only cheats on his wife and lies to his lover, whom he says he wants to move in with, but he also cheats on that woman with yet another. But was it different from having several casual sexual partners? On reflection she realised that in Bruno's case it was very different. In the first place, he had lied to her about being in a process of separation from his wife, he had lied about wanting them to live together as a couple, and he also had a third woman on the go, a woman who incredibly had turned out to be his first wife. He's a fantasist, she thought, maybe he even believes his own fantasies, and that's why he comes across as so convincing.

The story would lend itself either to a crime novel or just a book about a serial cheater, possibly a scammer. And it wasn't until that moment she realised that the Thailand holiday she and Bruno had planned had been paid for by her, when he mentioned the cost of living in two locations while his divorce was being finalised, so he really had scammed her.

Somehow this discovery made Saskia feel pleased, which seemed stranger still. She put aside the book she had been holding while sitting there thinking about Bruno, swung her legs out of bed and went into the living room with no particular aim in mind. Why did she feel vindicated by discovering her former lover had not only been a liar and a serial deceiver, but also a scammer? After a few minutes she laughed quietly, turned the light on and went to make herself a cup of tea. The answer had been hidden behind the layers of anger and resentment in her mind and having worked it out acted as a tonic. Of course, she thought, before I hit on the scam aspect I just felt like a gullible fool taken in by a handsome and amusing man, but now I feel I wasn't just easily fooled, I was taken for a ride by a criminal, a skilled and ruthless master of his craft. Which of course, makes me seem less like an idiot – what a nice feeling!

Back in her bed, her thoughts changed to her career, as if she had now discarded the emotional debris left from the break-up with Bruno. She hadn't yet told her agent that she was making a foray into a different genre and that she had already written two novels in what she thought of as the contemporary romance genre. Books for women about women, about their lives and loves and disappointments, but no detailed sex scenes as in the modern-day romance genre, which she thought of as "compensation porn". Last year when she had read a dozen modern romance novels to work out what the formula was, and check if she really wanted to write some, she mentioned this phrase to her friend Lizzie. And she had asked what it was compensation for, was it for readers who had no man in their lives, and Saskia said, "God no, they probably don't need compensation. I think it's for women with disappointing husbands, who never vary the routine or just go to sleep and snore, or who've become too unappealing – you know, guys who were medium attractive to start with and then got fat and slobby'.

Lizzie had looked hard at Saskia and said she thought just as many women got fat and slobby and were no longer enticing, as if she suspected Saskia of being sexist.

'No, listen - I think of it like this,' Saskia had explained. 'Men always had a ready fantasy remedy, it's called porn – in print form and now online. But until online porn became available there wasn't anything specifically for women, mostly it was aimed at men. And even these days I imagine many women wouldn't watch it online, so they read books that have a bit of softish porn in them, which are called romances. Or at least I think middle-aged women do. And that's their compensation.'

'It would be a huge change for you,' Lizzie had said, not responding directly to Saskia's explanation. 'You're so used to the crime aspect of your writing, isn't that how your mind works? Could you change?'

'I can't write that romance stuff I described, the compensation porn type. I'm simply not interested in writing books with those repetitive, detailed sex scenes, so I've put the idea on hold. The research I did put me off completely. The thought of having to introduce a sex scene every thirty pages or so, just makes me feel tired.'

This was, however, not quite true. She had already started writing her first contemporary women's novel before this conversation took place, but *sans* detailed sex scenes. Some kind of self-protective instinct had made her step back from confiding in Lizzie, as if she wanted to keep this development to herself for a while. She knew why, now that she had been doing it for a while longer and had just started on the third women's fiction novel. It was the pleasure of having an enjoyable thing to do that nobody asked about, like secretly eating chocolate, but in this case creative too. A private non-fattening treat, she told herself and laughed.

The Bruno story might lend itself better to one of her women's novels rather than crime, after all; it had all the right components. How could you go wrong with a scene like the one that took place when he came out of the shower that night? she thought, and how wonderful it would be on TV. It had all the components of a visually stunning confrontation; the furious woman, the handsome man who dropped his towel, the clothes thrown at his feet. She left the idea to develop in the back of her mind, knowing that one day it would pop up as if by magic with a lot of extra detail attached.

Matthew, her agent, knew only that she was busy writing the last book in her current thriller series, the third one set in the South Island, where she had introduced a secondary hero character. He might be disappointed when she told him she had also been writing these other books, but the fact that she hadn't told him had nothing to do with worry about what he would think. It was all to do with keeping it close to her heart for the sheer enjoyment of it.

Wide awake and full of plans, Saskia got out of

bed a second time and turned some lights on. Sitting at the breakfast counter with a second cup of tea forgotten in front of her, she explored this idea further. She always felt happy when writing in this new genre; it was so different, as far removed from crime writing as it was possible to get, perhaps with the exception of religious books. It flowed from her fingers to the keyboard, she laughed at times and enjoyed the company of her created characters. She sighed at their disappointments and imagined the comfort of their hugs. When she wrote crime she had none of those feelings, her mind was too preoccupied with the plot and the various details that led to a solution, the need to make the story credible and logical and get technical details right. She loved creating the crime novel character too, of course, and tried to make them three-dimensional with emotional depth, but there had been few over the years she had cared about in the same way. And in her women's books, she could make her characters do or say anything, however mad. If she decided they were a bit crazy and did or said unexpected and surprising things, then that's how it was.

If Matthew or her publisher didn't like them, she would change agents and leave the publishing firm. Her contract was about to be renewed, so it would be the perfect time for a change if they didn't want to handle her new books. Her crime novels were successful, two had been turned into TV series and she earned a lot of money from her ebooks, which sold continuously without any effort on her part. Matthew had only been her new agent for a couple of years, and though she liked him, she wouldn't hesitate to change. They would probably remain friends if she moved on, she thought, they got on so well and she was quite fond of him.

When Saskia finally went back to bed, her primary emotion was relief at having broken off with Bruno. The fact that until the very last few seconds of the confrontation she had not even raised her voice felt good. It was only that final moment when he tried to charm and caress his way past all her discoveries, when all she had wanted was for him to get out and leave her alone, that tipped her over the edge and set her screaming. Saskia smiled to herself when she recalled her earlier thought of the scene as part of a TV drama and realised that apart from anger and mortification at the deceit, she didn't care about Bruno at all.

She had an urge to tell someone what had happened, and Lizzie seemed like someone it would be safe to tell anything, unshockable and not a gossip. They had only known each other for a couple of years, after being introduced by Matthew, but they had become close friends surprisingly fast. Tomorrow was Tuesday, so Lizzie might be working a half day in the library, as she always did on the first two days of the week if she had worked the weekend. Saskia had never understood why Lizzie chose to work mornings on her half days, but that's what she did, worked in the morning as usual and had the afternoon off. She would text her in the morning and hopefully they would be able to meet for lunch somewhere.

Chapter 7

When Lizzie arrived at Sierra Café at half past one, she found Saskia at a table outside, reading on her Kindle and absent-mindedly stroking the head of a large black dog that sat beside her chair leaning against her leg.

'*Where* did you get that from?' said Lizzie in disbelief. 'Is it a rescue dog? Are you allowed dogs in your snazzy apartment block?'

'Oh, for heaven's sake, of course he's not mine, my flat isn't nearly large enough for a dog this big. I'm just looking after him while his owner gets coffee – he's called Napoleon, the dog I mean, I don't know what the owner's called.'

She smiled affectionately down at the dog, who reached up a paw and put it on her thigh. 'See? Isn't he the sweetest thing? He went straight to me when they arrived, just pulled the guy along at the end of his lead and sat down beside me. I think he likes my smell. We'll order as soon as the dog daddy comes back out.'

He turned up a couple of minutes later with a take-away mug of coffee, smiled at Lizzie and looked as if he would like to sit down and join them, but Saskia said, 'I'm sorry, but you can't join us. It would have been nice to have Napoleon for a little longer, but I'm going to tell my friend the torrid details of breaking up with my lover last night, so we need privacy.'

'Awesome!' said the man and took Napoleon's lead from Saskia. 'Have fun!'

The dog turned his head and looked back at Saskia as they walked away, and she waved at him. 'Gorgeous!' she said. 'He really and truly loved me, not like that bastard Bruno.'

Sitting there in the shade of a large sun umbrella, at their favourite table where they had sat several times this hot summer with the breeze from the harbour sweeping gently past, the story Saskia was about to tell seemed surreal.

'Did you? Break up with Bruno, I mean? You weren't just saying it to get rid of the dog daddy? What happened?'

When Saskia nodded and said yes, Lizzie didn't look quite as surprised as Saskia had thought she would, because Lizzie's face was always very expressive. 'Several reasons – let me tell you what happened.'

She stirred half a straw of sugar into her coffee and held up her hand to count on her fingers with the spoon. 'Number one – he's not in the middle of a divorce, he's still happily married. Two – he's not childless, he has three young children, two girls and a boy. Three – his flat in town is just a five day a week thing for work, and the family live in a lovely house on Waiheke Island. Four – he's the most talented, believable and creative liar I've ever met, and five – he also has an *ex-wife* and goes to visit her in Morningside to have sex a couple of times a month. And she sends him filthy selfies as a reward. Enough?'

'Are you kidding?' said Lizzie and started to laugh. 'Sorry to laugh, but it's just too much. How upset *are* you?'

'I was upset for a few minutes, very upset - now I'm mainly angry with myself for not catching on earlier. I've kind of realised since I threw him out last night that I didn't love him, I just liked him and wanted him, like you want something shiny and new that others might envy, perhaps. *Not* the same thing as love! I confronted him, after he turned up at nine and went straight to have a shower in my lovely bathroom, saying he'd been out running and not cooled off for long enough before getting dressed. I told you he was a talented creative liar, didn't I? But the truth was that he had come straight from his ex-wife and some steamy sex, the first wife, I mean, after leaving his loving family on Waiheke early on some pretext, so he could fit us all into his busy bonking schedule.'

She drank some of her coffee and noticed Lizzie's expression of anticipation as if she could nearly sense the dramatic ending. 'Anyway, he'd left his phone unlocked on the kitchen counter when he arrived – I think he must have read his current wife's text in the lift. Then a text ping came when he'd just got into the shower, and I didn't know if it was a text or a call alert, so I picked up the phone.'

She chuckled. 'It was a text that read "thanks for fabulous sex just now, maybe I shouldn't have divorced you, haha." So, I opened some messages from his primary school age kids, some from his current wife in the big house on Waiheke, all of which were signed with kisses, and a few more from the ex-wife. That's when I saw the truly disgusting photos she sends him.'

'What did you do?' Lizzie's eyes were wide and hungry for details, and Saskia suddenly wondered if this was what Lizzie's life was made up of. Other people's dramas and romances and disappointments, things that probably most of her friends felt comfortable to tell her.

'I kind of went into super-fast planning mode – not something I've ever had to do before, but I think I did it quite well, all things considered. First I texted the wife's phone number from his phone to mine, not to use, you understand, just to have as a threat for him to sweat about. Then I changed his lock code, closed the phone and waited until he came out, wrapped in one of my new super-soft yellow towels, heading towards me for a hug and a smooch like he usually does after a shower. He loves, I mean loved, that little act of letting the towel slip and standing there in his naked glory, the lying bastard. He's quite fond of his physique.'

She laughed at the memory, surprised herself by how comic it now seemed, like something she had seen on TV or read about. 'He didn't know what was happening, it was quite funny. I evaded the hug and walked around him to the bathroom, picked up his clothes and threw them at his feet and said, Get dressed and get out! Right now.' She made a face at the memory of what followed. 'I'll spare you the pleading and the lying and the attempts to calm me down, his choice of words, not mine. I was quietly furious, but I'm proud to say I was in total control until the very last moment.'

Lizzie was giggling continuously now and getting red in the face. 'And then?'

'I told him I knew he's a lying cheat, and I wanted him out faster than fast. He got dressed, put the phone in his pocket and continued trying to sweet talk me into "telling him what was wrong" – his choice of phrase. As if I hadn't already spelled it out in capital letters. So I went to the front door, and he followed, and then he tried to grab me in a hug. So, I yelled at him to get out of my sight and held the door open. And he left.'

'Have you heard anything from him since?'

'Nope. He can't call me until he gets another phone or borrows one, and he probably doesn't know my number by heart anyway. I've changed my PIN for the downstairs door, I got the building manager to do it first thing this morning - we all have our own PIN to get in if we don't have our swipe card with us. And if he sends an email about his phone I'll say get back to me in a couple of days because I can't remember the PIN I put on it, which isn't true. It's his birthday date – day and month, so he might figure it out eventually. And don't worry, I'm not going to tell his wife, I just texted her number from his phone to myself for him to see and sweat about.'

'So, no trip to Thailand, or maybe he'll take his wife or ex-wife instead.' Lizzie got up. 'This is so damn exciting I need to pee. Back in a moment – I've got something to tell you.'

'No trip to Thailand for *him*,' said Saskia with great satisfaction when Lizzie returned. 'But there's another thing I should tell you, which made me feel better and a lot less like a silly fool. He really is a conman, and it wasn't just the lies about his life. He said he couldn't afford to go to Thailand because of having to pay for his flat in town as well as all costs for where he had lived with his wife until the divorce was final – this was before I knew about this big house at

Waiheke, so I paid for us both! He scammed me! Maybe you'd like to come with me? It's booked for early June around the time of my birthday.'

'I would have loved to,' said Lizzie. 'We've never been away together, I bet we'd have fun! But my parents are coming out from England at the end of April, remember, and now they've decided they'll be staying for three months, not just six weeks. We're going to tour the South Island for three weeks in June – they want to see the snow on the southern alps and all that. I did warn them there'll be a lot of wind and rain as well, and the snow comes later and later each year, but they say they don't mind. We've got one of those giant motor homes booked, which I'll have to drive, damn it!'

'And what were you going to tell me?' asked Saskia before they parted. 'You said something when you dashed off to the toilet and then we never got back to it, because I was on a roll with the Bruno drama, sorry!'

'Oh, yes – I was surprised at the depth of deception on Bruno's part, but I had kind of been expecting something to emerge about him. Marian said something not long after their Christmas event that made me wonder if she knew something about him.'

'Really? What did she say?' Saskia found this revelation surprising and slightly worrying. 'Why didn't she tell me whatever she knew?'

'Oh, it might just have been a rumour – I don't know. She didn't say anything specific, she just made a passing comment like "she'll get tired of him, he's not in her class, he's got a reputation" or something like it. And I'd already noticed that you didn't like being asked about him, which seemed a bit odd, but I reckoned if there was something weird going on you would have said.'

This lowkey and undemanding statement made Saskia feel guilty and she put her hand on Lizzie's arm and said, 'I should have, and I probably would have sooner or later. But at the time it was just a vague feeling of not being quite comfortable introducing him to friends. Which *should* have made me consider why I felt that way. It's surely the best indicator ever that you should get rid of someone fast.'

'You said he was very entertaining and handsome, so it might have been a hard choice,' said Lizzie in a comforting voice, but Saskia shook her head. 'No, I was just indecisive and a bit silly, and I'll know better next time. Being handsome and charming and amusing is definitely not the same thing as being a good or even medium good person.'

That evening Bruno called just when the light was changing to the golden tint she loved because it made her entire living room glow. After nearly not picking up the call from an unknown number, she felt guilty when she heard who it was. Though Bruno obviously had access to another phone, the matter of the locked phone was beginning to make her feel that she had been vindictive, which was not a characteristic she felt comfortable with.

'Yes?' she said instead of her usual greeting when he said who it was. Nothing more, just the one word and there was a pause before he spoke.

'Please let me in,' he said in that velvety, caressing voice she knew so well. 'I can explain everything, please don't be cross. We can sort this out, honey.'

'Where are you?'

'Right beneath your balcony.'

He actually expected her to let him in! Saskia shook her head in disbelief and thought, not for the first time since she threw him out, that he was a master of self-deception as well as having a lot of other nasty traits.

Saskia went out on the balcony and looked down, and there he was looking up at her, and in her ear his voice continued trying to sway her, telling her he didn't know what he would do without her. It was odd to hear his voice from two directions, but she kept the phone to her ear. Leaning on the balcony rail, she said very loudly, as if she wasn't still holding the phone, 'You actually thought I'd let you in if you came around? You clearly have no sense of proportion, Bruno, and nobody ever told you the meaning of the word no. So, listen to what I'm about to tell you! I'm not angry, I'm just over you, totally over you. There isn't the slightest chance that I'll let you into my life again. It's partially my own fault for being so gullible and not noticing what a lying shit you are, I really should have picked up on it ages ago.'

'We can fix this, darling,' said Bruno smoothly, looking up at her and also speaking loudly, as if neither of them had phones in their hands. How odd, thought Saskia, it's like one person has tricked the other one into talking louder, but unintentionally, it's as if we feel we have to talk loudly because we can see each other even though we're on the phone.

'If we sit down and talk about it we can sort it out. I couldn't get in - your door code didn't work and then some big ape came along and refused to let me in and told me to fuck off. But you know what we have is worth saving, it's such a great relationship.'

He was on a roll now, hoping to wear her resistance down, but why? Why not just give up? Was it that he couldn't get into his own phone, or did his ego not allow him to give in too easily? Was he one of those self-centred people who feel they should do the breaking up?

'There is no relationship,' she said calmly, but still loudly. 'I'll tell you what I changed your lock PIN to, the one for your own phone, so you can use it again. I only did that to make you worry a bit. But before I tell you what the new PIN is I'd like you to know this, just to have it on record and for you to think about. I heard the ping on your phone last night and I thought I'd take a call for you while you were in the shower, but it was a text message from you *first* wife, thanking you for the steamy sex you two had an hour earlier. No wonder you needed a shower! And I did note the dirty pictures she sends you – truly disgusting. So, then I looked at Wendy's texts – your current wife, I mean, the one you pretend you're in the process of divorcing. Do you remember her? She's that one who lives on Waiheke Island. And I found that she sent a fond farewell when you got on the ferry at four yesterday afternoon and she signed it with three kisses. And I also noticed the pictures she sends you nearly every day of what your three children are up to during the day – you know those kids you and Wendy don't have, or so you said. So, thank you for taking such long showers, it gave me lots of time to have a good look.'

She paused for a moment. What else would she like to tell him? Ah, yes – this would be a good farewell note. 'And listen, Bruno – another thing before I give you the new code for your phone. When you get into it you'll see you sent me a text last night with your wife's phone number. Such a thoughtful thing to do! The new **PIN** is the first four numbers in your birth date, day followed by month.'

She closed the call and went inside and felt a weight slide from her shoulders. To have been able to calmly and clinically list all she had found on his phone made her feel more like her normal self, as if the screaming harridan, who had ordered him out of her flat, had been consigned to the rubbish bin and was no longer sitting like a dark stain in her mind. She had joked about it when she told Lizzie the story, but she was not proud of herself for that outburst. She wondered vaguely who it might have been who had refused to let him into the building. Some big ape, he had said, possibly a visitor who had a tenant's code and wasn't comfortable about letting someone in. And thank goodness for that, she thought, as she turned on the lights in the living room, or I might have opened the door and found him on the doorstep.

With a mug of tea and her Kindle she spent a couple of hours in someone else's world, living the life of their characters, happily immersed in their story, and when she went to bed that night the entire Bruno episode had been relegated to the storage section of her mind, where things that no longer had the power to touch her gathered dust.

Chapter 8

As soon as Saskia spotted Ross in the international arrivals hall at Auckland airport she had a feeling that something was wrong, and her imagination went into instant overdrive listing what it might be. Serious illness, redundancy (could a professor be made redundant?), lost all his savings in a scam, killed someone on the road in an accident? When they hugged and she uttered the conventional and usually meaningless phrase, 'How are you?' she found herself emphasising *are*, and when he replied that he was fine, and how was she, she stood back and looked searchingly at him.

'Something's wrong.' She tried to smile. 'You can't hide anything from me, you know that - you never could. I developed psychic powers at the age of four. What is it?'

'OK,' he said. 'Something strange happened, but

nothing's wrong. It's more like I worry about telling you because it concerns you. But this isn't the place – let's wait until we get back to your place.'

As she drove back to the city he told her about the latest finds at the dig at Oenpelli in the Northern Territory, the site he had worked on for several years during the university holidays. 'Did I mention we found some more axe heads? No? They're probably about twenty-five thousand years old, nicely shaped too, one with a ground edge. But Kimberly has the world record for a ground-edge axe, a hafted one – more than forty-five thousand years. Oldest of its kind in the world.'

As always when he talked about archaeological finds, he sounded more animated than at any other time. She glanced at him. 'Hafted means with a handle, right? It's such a great word, I must find a way to use it in a book.'

She knew he would grin at that. He had always enjoyed what he called her vocab collection, and since age seven or eight she had kept a series of notebooks that she gradually filled with interesting words, phrases and sometimes whole sentences.

'Put it in your notebook as soon as we get home,' he said now. 'I presume you still do it?'

'Oh yes, I've never stopped, and I still have the whole collection, right from that first one. Remember the one with the shiny pink vinyl cover you bought me for a birthday? I wrote up a great phrase the other week, but I haven't found a way to use it yet. Listen to this: Her gaze skated smoothly over the planes of his face like a ballerina on ice, did a pirouette on his forehead and came to rest on his eyes. Isn't it marvellous, I can't wait to use it!'

Now he laughed outright. 'Perfect! Where did you find that?'

'Oh, just in my little writer's brain,' she said, pretend-modestly. 'Every now and then I think of something ridiculous or clever, or funny, and if I didn't write it down I'd never remember. Just the other day I read that some writers keep a notebook and pen on their bedside table and if something occurs to them in the night, they turn the light on and write it down. I haven't got to that stage yet, but there's no saying I won't one day.'

As soon as the door was closed behind them, Saskia poured them an earlier than usual glass of white wine and opened to the door to the balcony.

'Now,' she said and ushered her father through the door. 'Would you please sit down and tell me what this is about, this thing that concerns me. I can't possibly settle down to anything until I've heard what it is.'

For the first time in her life, Saskia's father said he didn't know where to start, which made her laugh, despite how tense she felt.

'Remember what you used to tell me when I told you about things that happened at school, all in the wrong order and having to back-track? Do the Alice thing.'

'Ah, yes, of course - I'll do the Alice thing,' said Ross. 'I'll start at the beginning, continue until I get to the end and then stop.' He sounded as if he was still stalling, then he cleared his throat.

'Well, here we go then. I was clearing out the big walk-in hall cupboard in my flat a couple of days ago and I found a box I hadn't looked at for ages. I've been having a sorting and discarding binge because I've got far too much old stuff I never use. I didn't recognise the box, one of those shallow white document boxes. I'd put it on the top shelf and then other things ended up on top of it, so I thought it had probably been sitting there since I moved to Sydney eighteen years ago. And when I took it down to see what was in it I had the surprise of my life.'

He drank some of his wine and shook his head at how remiss he had been. 'It was much older than eighteen years, more like thirty-something. It was from when we moved house here in Auckland when you were about six or seven – remember how we moved from the one-bedroom flat to a slightly bigger one so you could have your own room? We'd left the last bit of packing a bit late, so we did it in a hurry the night before the removal truck came, and there was more to do than we had counted on.'

Saskia nodded without replying. That last frantic evening of packing things into whatever they could find was clear in her mind. She had eventually fell asleep in an armchair, and Ross covered her with a blanket and didn't wake her up until the next morning, just before the movers arrived.

'I must have just stuffed a last papers from my desk into that box,' said Ross. 'The things that were left after I packed all my uni papers into those big boxes the moving company gave us. And somehow this one never got looked at again. In it wasn't only old bank statements and a used-up cheque book – remember those? There were two unopened envelopes too that had probably come in the mail the previous day, that's how I know how old that box was, and also an envelope I'd got out to show you on your birthday that year. And then I thought you were too young and decided to keep it until you were a bit older, so I left it on the desk, and it got buried. When I looked for it a couple of years later, I couldn't find it and I thought I'd lost it in the move.'

He put his hand in his back pocket and brought out a square envelope roughly the size of a birthday card, now slightly curved and crushed looking. On the front was his name but no address.

'This,' he said seriously, 'is the letter that came with you. Tucked in beside you in your little Moses basket. It's from your mother.'

If the silence that followed had taken on physical form and shape it would have been the colour and weight of a small block of granite, heavy and hard to move. After a long silence Saskia reached out and he handed the envelope to her, but she didn't open it.

'Tucked into the basket?' she said. 'Did she really come and give me to you in a basket? She didn't hold me?'

'I never saw her at all that day.' Ross spoke slowly, his focus on the past, re-living the memory. 'We'd agreed I would take charge of you from the end of week three, which was when we thought we should have been able to get the birth registered and all the formalities organised. We hadn't seen each other for months. She went to stay with someone, and I had no idea where she was, she wouldn't tell me. Remember this was before everyone had cell phones. She called one evening, probably from the phone box on the street corner by my little flat, to check if I was at home. She said she'd be there in roughly half an hour and to stay home, so she didn't miss me. Half an hour later she called again and said, "come to your front door". I was on the ground floor in a block of eight little flats on a quiet street near the university, a tiny studio flat, which you won't remember. I moved away from there a couple of months later, it was just too small for the two of us.'

Saskia sat mesmerised with her eyes fixed on his face, waiting for the last piece of this mesmerising tale that she had never heard before.

'I opened the door,' said Ross quietly, 'and there you were, on the hall floor outside my door, in the little basket. And beside you sat a large suitcase with everything you needed. If I'd had a smartphone then I would have taken a photo of the scene – it was like something out of a movie. You were tucked in with a pink blanket, sound asleep, with one tiny hand curled beside your face. I'd never seen anything to pretty in my life. And in the suitcase was every single thing I would need for the next fortnight at least. I had no clue about how to look after you apart from what I'd read in a baby book I got from the library. I'd never even held a baby, or any small child for that matter.'

'And that was the last you heard from her?' asked Saskia, fascinated and slightly outraged by the chilly efficiency of her mother. 'You never got to say goodbye or anything?'

'No, nothing further, not a thing. And, of course, I didn't see her that day. I think she made the first call from the phone box and then she unloaded everything when the coast was clear and watched from the phone box after she made the second call. I reconstructed it afterwards, knowing what a planner she was. She would have had someone to drive her, she didn't have a car. And she'd probably predicted that I'd come straight out on the street and look both ways and that would, of course, tell her I'd found you, that you were safe.'

'And this?' asked Saskia without opening the envelope. 'It's got your name on it.'

'Read it,' he said and sat back with his wine glass,

his focus fully on the present again. 'Do you want me to go inside, so you can look at in private?'

'For God's sake, dad - of course, not! We've been a team since that day and we're still a team, even if we live in different countries now.'

She pulled out the tucked-in flap and pulled out a white card, which looked like the plain half of a birthday card.

Dear Ross, here is Saskia and all her bits and pieces. Feeding schedule and how to mix feeds on the separate sheet and also the birth certificate. I'm going back to the US very soon. Please give her all she needs and love her. Amanda

'It must have been painful for her,' said Ross. 'I don't know how long she spent deciding what to do after I managed to persuade her not to have an abortion and said if she had the baby I'd bring it up, which I did as soon as I realised she wanted a termination. But weighing up what to do – such a hard decision to have to make.'

Saskia studied his sun-browned, creased face while a stream of thoughts ran through her mind. What a compassionate man he was, to feel pity for a woman who first wanted to get rid of his baby, then decided her career came first and left her baby behind with a boy not quite twenty-one. How lucky she was to have a father like that, who from that day on hardy ever went out and rarely dated, so he could be a proper parent, how he must have struggled at times, juggling studies and a baby. Admittedly with help from a creche, his mother and an aunt, but she had aways known where she belonged, with her young father in whatever little flat they were living in at the time.

'You did such a great job,' she said and reached across the table to grip his hand. 'I had the best childhood and the best parent. Sometimes people ask me if I miss not having a mother, and I always say I don't, and it's true – I never felt I needed one.'

Before they went to bed that first night her father said, 'Do you still sing?' and Saskia smiled, remembered how he had offered her professional singing lessons when she was a teenager and how disappointed he had been that she had turned to offer down. He used to say it was a gift to have a voice like hers, and it should be used. But she had never felt like singing as a career, all she ever wanted to do was write.

'Oh yes, I do sing, usually to myself in the car and sometimes in the shower. I sing to my goddaughter, Anna, and sometimes I sing in the lift. Really any time apart from when I'm writing - then all I want is perfect silence.'

Chapter 9

Some weeks later Saskia stood in her kitchen with a half-made sandwich in front of her on the bench. Her hand holding the cheese slicer lay idle beside the slice of bread as if someone had left it there and forgotten about it. She stared vacantly at nothing, deep in thought about the book she had been working on since that morning. She knew she should have been working to finish the third crime novel in the series, which had a deadline coming up quite soon, but she hadn't been able to resist the temptation to continue her secret project.

It was exciting to have something to work on that made her feel so upbeat and cheerful, something so utterly removed from what she had been writing for more than a decade. Somehow inventing the stories in her growing line-up of women's fiction novels came naturally to her, without effort and the way she could twist the story line and deviate from what had been her initial intention was such fun. Nothing she made her characters do or say, and nothing she invented at the spur of a moment could ruin the plot in the same way it might in a crime novel where details and facts had to fit and make sense to the critical reader.

It's such a relief, she thought, and finally cut a slice of cheese for her sandwich. It's taken science and hard facts and strict logic out of writing and turned it into pure fun. I can make my characters be outrageous or silly or do any kind of stupid thing. If I say my central woman character is a bit random and says crazy things at times and embarrasses herself, well, then that's how she is. I created her and she can do what she likes. This was a concept she frequently returned to, the creative freedom of the new genre, and in her heart she knew she might never write another crime novel. And even if her current editor accepted these new books, which was doubtful, she knew she would have a battle on her hands to make her accept that the characters were not to be changed. She could just imagine Audrey saying, 'Would anyone really say that to a man she's just met? Isn't it a bit odd, a bit abrupt? I want you to change it.'

And Saskia pictured herself looking Audrey in the eye saying, 'Nope, she's an entertaining and clever woman, who sometimes says random things that sound nearly shocking, so if that's what she said, then that's how it is.' And that would lead to a battle that Saskia would probably lose.

She sat down in front of her laptop and started reading the two thousand words she had written since breakfast, changing a detail here and there, and once laughing out loud, and then her phone rang.

'Hi,' said Audrey briskly. 'How's the book going? Will you be finished on time?'

'Oh, I think so,' said Saskia and smiled to herself. 'I've had a wonderful morning and I've written two thousand words since breakfast.'

'Oh, great!' said Audrey sounding relieved. 'Remember that I need to have it before the end of April, so we can start working on it. I'll send you a couple of images we're thinking of for the cover.'

No need to tell her the two thousand words aren't for the book she's waiting for, thought Saskia, and reached for her mug. What she doesn't know, won't hurt her. Aloud she said, 'I'll get it to you by the deadline, no trouble. I'll have it done in a couple of weeks or maybe four. And why are you showing me images of the cover already? You don't even know the full plot yet.'

'Oh, the detail doesn't matter,' said Audrey breezily, making Saskia feel as if her efforts counted for nothing. 'You sent me a vague outline a few months ago, remember? We've based it on that and the first two covers and kind of taken it a step further, so they'll look great lined up beside each other. I'll send them over later today.'

When they ended the call Saskia sat for a moment trying to analyse why the prospect of seeing what the publishers had dreamed up for the cover didn't make her feel the usual mixture of apprehension and seething impotence. She had no real power to reject a cover and only limited opportunity to ask for changes, and in the past it had frustrated her. While she was writing she built a complete world in her head and knew what everyone looked like, what their environment was like and, most importantly, that elusive thing she thought of as the atmosphere of the book. And then they presented her with a cover image that clashed with her mental image, and it felt as if someone had corrupted her creation. But now she didn't feel like that, and she wondered why.

It's because I really don't care, she thought suddenly and laughed. They can do what they like with it. I don't care, it's my last crime novel and it doesn't matter. Maybe it would be fun to think of covers for my new books instead, in case I decide to self-publish them, try to decide on some kind of theme, an overall look that would tie them together, show they're by the same author and in the same genre.

She opened her internet browser and started searching Amazon for books similar to her own new novels and found that a lot of them had a cover image of a woman, with detailed backgrounds and often with the title in fancy script. She didn't want fussy or messy, she wanted crisp, attractive and minimal, and definitely not cartoon style drawings. Recalling that someone had mentioned a site called Shutterstock, she looked it up and spent the next two hours immersed in gorgeous photos of nature and art works and abstract patterns, most of them available to buy and use as book covers.

'It's a treasure trove,' she said to Marian in phone call at the end of the day. 'You just can't imagine it until you've seen it. Millions of photos to choose from, but I think I've cracked it.'

'But what's it for?' asked Marian. 'Are they letting you have a say in the cover design this time? I didn't think they ever did that.'

And Saskia remembered that she hadn't even told Marian about her secret writing project, which made her feel guilty and she wondered why she hadn't. Marian was her oldest and closest friend after all, not someone she had ever hid anything from. But it was the same thing as with Lizzie, the urge to keep it secret, her hidden fun. Because thar's what it was, that feeling she got when she was writing these new books, the creative freedom made her happy. A lovely, relaxing little adventure that beckoned her away from her crime novel at least once a week and which tended wrap itself around her until she surfaced hours later, dazed and happy. I think I get drunk on words, she silently told herself, I don't need wine when I write these new books.

'I'm only telling you, not anyone else yet,' she said. 'I haven't even told my agent or anyone at the publishers. It's such fun and I don't want them to start throwing cold water on it and ruin how much I'm enjoying it. It's a book in a different genre. About women, adult women, not girls.'

'With a love story? Or just about life in general?' asked Marian and then there was a loud crash and she shouted, 'Oh, bugger! Sorry, must go!'

Thoughtful and slightly worried, Saskia sat with the phone still in her hand and tried to identify what it was Marian had said somewhere during their short conversation that had given her the impression that something was wrong. Or maybe it wasn't anything she had said, it might have been something in her tone of voice. They had been friends for so many years and mostly discussed everything that went on in their lives; she felt sure she hadn't imagined a slight nuance of trouble. Money, illness, work problems? she wondered, or something going wrong in their marriage. She was well aware that however well you knew someone, there would be things going on in the background that outsiders could not see.

Chapter 10

Not long before midnight one evening at the beginning of March, an unusual sound made Saskia look up and mute the TV. It wasn't a sound she had heard before, a distant, but insistent high-pitched beeping, perhaps some kind of alarm signal. She got up and walked around trying to identify where it was coming from. In the hallway the sound got louder and when she opened her from door she was confronted by something that looked like a scene in a TV drama.

Her neighbour was lying on his back with most of his body out on the landing, his head was surrounded by a pool of blood and his lower legs blocked the lift doors. Unconscious, she thought and only us on this level at the moment with the Chambers on the other side of me away, so nobody available to help me. Thought and ideas raced through her head as she ran back into her flat to grab her phone and a clean kitchen towel. She stood still for only the second it took to dial 111, then she ran back to the lift.

'No, I can't leave him,' she said to the emergency call centre after giving her name and address. 'He's hit his head quite badly, and I think I'd better try to staunch the blood flow, so I can't go down and let them in – we're on level three and it would take too long. If I give you my keypad PIN for the street door, can you pass it on to them? And maybe my phone number as well, just in case. And tell them to press button three in the lift.'

'Keep the call open,' said the operator. 'Put the phone on speaker and put it near you – we might need to give you instructions.'

She put the phone on the floor, stepped over the man's legs and managed to slide them out of the way of the lift door. As soon as his legs no longer blocked the door it closed, the beeping stopped, and the lift returned to the ground floor with a quiet hiss.

Kneeling beside her unconscious neighbour she folded the towel into a thick pad and held it against the side of his head where the blood seemed to be coming from. 'I hope I've got the right spot,' she whispered to herself and applied pressure with the other hand on the opposite side of his head, 'but it's hard to see with so much blood everywhere and this thick hair, it's like a bear's pelt. Please hurry up, ambulance, please! And please, what's-your-name, please don't die!'

She took a deep breath and steadied herself, told herself to calm down and be sensible. 'Oh, of course I know, I'm just a bit shocked' she whispered a moment later. 'Your name is Dankworth, it's on your mailbox downstairs in the lobby, it's next to mine. You're Orson Dankworth. I must remember to tell the ambulance people.'

Orson's eyelids fluttered as if he had reacted to hearing his name, and for a short moment he looked right up at her face, then they closed again.

'Orson,' she said, bending low over his face, hoping it was his name that had roused him. 'Orson, listen! You're going to be OK, the ambulance is coming, and they'll know what to do, we'll just have to wait a little while.'

Time seemed to move at a snail's pace as she knelt with her hands pressed against the sides of his head like the two sides of a vice. If only the neighbours on her other side weren't away! She could shout, but shouting wouldn't reach the next floor down, and people were probably asleep anyway. Not that there was anything anyone could do, apart from what she was already doing, but she felt insecure alone with a man who might be dying. Then she heard squawking noises from the phone she had forgotten about and called out, 'Can you speak louder, really loud. I can't hear you. I forgot to put it on speaker and now I can't let go of his head to move the phone closer.'

The operator raised her voice. 'Is he still unconscious?'

'Yes, but he opened his eyes a few minutes ago, just for a moment.'

'Is he breathing OK? Do you know how to take his pulse?'

'I have no idea, and I can't let go of his head, or he'll lose even more blood, he's lost a lot already. His breathing seems normal. How far away is the ambulance?'

'Four or five minutes,' said the voice. 'Just hang in there, you're doing a great job - they'll soon be there and take over.'

Random thoughts appeared in Saskia's head as looked down as Orson: how unfair it was of nature to give such luscious eyelashes to a man, and maybe he had got paler since she found him, was it from the blood loss or did he have a bad head injury, hopefully her phone wouldn't go flat before the ambulance got there, the battery was very, very low, and what was that strange feeling she was getting, like an insistent urge in the back of her head that he needed protection or support. She shook her head and dismissed the thought as a reaction to an injured fellow being and shuffled closer on her knees, so she didn't need to lean forward all the time with her arms outstretched, because now her back was beginning to protest.

· · ·

'His name is Orson Dankworth,' said Saskia when the ambulance crew stepped out of the lift carrying cases and a folded gurney. 'What do you need to know?'

'Any medical issues?' asked the woman, who was kneeling on the floor opening a case, without looking up. 'Age, address, marital status?'

'I'm his cousin,' said Saskia impulsively, struck by sudden inspiration and determined to stay in the picture. She couldn't bear the thought that these people would take him away. She felt a need to create a connection of some kind, however fictitious, to keep herself involved. A cousin would be a close enough relative to be granted rights, surely, but a bit more detail might add weight.

'We've only just recently kind of discovered each other, we never met until a few weeks ago. I think he's forty-two or maybe forty-three. He was coming to stay, and he was late, so I was getting worried, and then I heard a bang and the lift beeping and beeping, so I came out to see what was going on and found him lying here bleeding – and blocking the lift door from closing.'

She pointed the wide square pillar beside the lift. 'You can see where he hit his head – that mark wasn't there before. He must have tripped or fainted or something.'

Twenty minutes later they were getting ready to leave. The white neck brace they had put on Orson when they first arrived pushed his chin up and the bandage around his head came down to his black eyebrows, and Saskia thought it looked as if he were looking out between two wide slats in a blind, though his eyes were closed, of course.

'Hang on, don't leave without me,' she said, without asking if they minded. 'I'll just grab my bag and come with you instead of driving behind you.'

That way I'll be right there instead of trying to get access to him once they've taken him behind the scenes, she thought, as she hurried back into her apartment, blessing the chance that had made her sit up late binge-watching a rerun of the first season of Killing Eve.

Sliding out of her bloodied track pants and leaving them on the bathroom floor, she quickly washed her hands and knees, threw the facecloth in the basin and pulled jeans over her still pink knees. Grabbing her shoulder bag and phone charger she put her keys in her pocket and was out on the landing closing her door before the ambulance crew had even finished packing up their gear.

Chapter 11

The ambulance bay and inner parts of the emergency department were busy, but nothing seemed desperately urgent. Nobody she could see was bleeding heavily, no staff rushed trolleys past at a run, and the patients she could see were conscious. Orson was efficiently wheeled along to a curtained cubicle on one side the central area where computers and desks were crowded in. Normally Saskia would have taken it all in, made mental notes for possible future use in a book, and asked a few questions, but tonight her whole attention was on Orson.

She followed the gurney into the cubicle, put her bag on the floor beside a chair in the corner and took a couple of steps closer to Orson, but a woman's voice stopped her. 'Could you please step back for a moment,' said a nurse who had now joined the ambulance crew. 'We need to transfer him from the gurney. Please sit on that chair, and you'll be able to see what we're doing.'

Saskia watched fascinated as Orson was swiftly moved to the bed or table in the middle of the space, how three gloved pairs of hands rolled him on his side, the way they all seemed to know what each one was doing and what to do next. It's like ballet, she thought, just a few brief words calmly spoken now and then, everyone's synchronised. She never took her eyes off Orson, or what she could see of him. The ambulance crew left, an older woman with a nametag that said she was a doctor came in with a razor and a pair of scissors in a paper packet in her gloved hands. Sterile, of course, thought Saskia, and watched one nurse hold his head tilted, while chunks of thick black hair matted with congealing blood were cut off and then the buzz of the electric razor. The doctor bent to looks closely at Orson's head, the side away from Saskia which was probably a good thing; she had never seen a bad wound and she wouldn't like to embarrass herself by fainting. The doctor blotted blood from Orson's head and her hand moved over his skull, back and forth, then she said, 'I'll put stitches in now or he'll bleed right through the scan. Let's hope we don't have to take them out again.'

Of course, thought Saskia, they'll do a scan to check if his skull is fractured, and maybe to check that his neck isn't damaged. I noticed how carefully they supported his head when they removed that neck brace thing and tilted his head.

With the stitching done, the doctor turned back to Saskia. 'If you go and sit in the waiting area just over there to the right, we'll get an orderly to take him to radiology for a scan. We'll tell you as soon as he's back here. There's a coffee machine in the waiting area, and sandwiches in the little fridge.

Saskia was reluctant to let them take Orson away without her, but something about the doctor's voice made it clear that going with him was not an option. Obediently she picked up her bag and stood waiting until an orderly turned up, when she managed to briefly touch Orson's hand as he was wheeled away and went to sit by the coffee machine. Leaning her head against the wall, she closed her eyes and sighed. I hope they don't hurt him when they do the scan, she thought, and what if he wakes up inside one of those tunnel shaped scan machines? He might panic and then what would happen? But all she could do was wait. She read the instructions about handwashing taped to the wall, and got her phone out to mute it, in case it let out one her alert signals. Every so often the door just along from where she was sitting opened and another patient was brought through from the public waiting area, sometimes a variety of family members followed and went to clutter up the cubicles, and she wondered how staff could function in what must often be a crowded and chaotic environment.

A woman in a white shirt instead of scrubs came over, perched on the edge of the chair next to Saskia and handed her a clipboard with a pen attached with a grubby string.

'You came in with Mr Dankworth, I believe, and you're his cousin? OK, can you please sign this form, seeing he's not conscious. It authorises us to operate if necessary and to give him a blood transfusion if it should be needed. We've looked him up in our system, so we know which medical clinic he goes to, but he's not got any next of kin listed and no emergency contacts.'

Saskia took the clipboard and promised to return it when the form was completed, and the woman went back to the central area. The form had been printed from computerised records and had all Orson's personal data, so having appointed herself to cousin status Saskia thought she would discover all she could. At some stage she might need to know something, to prove she really was his cousin, so she started reading.

Orson Dankworth was four years older than Saskia, and his occupation was mysteriously listed as hedge fund manager. Hedge fund? Over the years she had read and heard the phrase many times, but she was vague about the specifics. Some kind of fund for hedging your bets when you invested, she imagined, perhaps to make a profit if exchange rates changed? Deciding to research it on her phone later, she continued reading all the data on the form and noted that Orson suffered from hypotension, which meant low blood pressure, so that might explain why he fell.

Saskia was nearly at the barrier around the central area, where she could see the blond woman talking to someone, when she had an idea. She stopped halfway and holding the clipboard awkwardly with one hand she fished her phone out of her pocket and quickly created a new contact. Only when she had entered Orson's phone number and birth date into her phone did she walk forward and put the clipboard on top of the barrier and waited as the woman approached. She picked up the clipboard and flicked to the second page and said, 'You haven't signed it,' and passed it back.

'Sorry,' said Saskia. I'm so worried about Orson I can't really concentrate – he's my only cousin.'

She wrote her name in capitals where indicated, filled in her own phone number, and signed on the dotted line, before she returned to her chair. Was she particularly good at lying? Or was she good at this because she was so used to inventing dialogue out of thin air? It was an unexpected talent that she had never had to resort to before and very useful right now, but why was she doing this at all? Until that moment she hadn't considered why she was so obsessed with not letting Orson out of her sight, to be right there, as close as they'd let her, and not leave him alone. But no explanation came to her, and the more she pondered, the more unreal it seemed. Here was a man she had only ever exchanged four or five words with, who had never smiled at her or even shown any sign he particularly noticed her in the lift lobby or the underground car parking area. It's very strange, she thought, but did it matter why she felt like this? The main thing now was to make sure he wasn't alone, and if some genuine cousin or other relative turned up she would just melt into the background and go home.

Time passed, two older women came to sit alongside her, one of them kept sniffling and saying, 'I *told* him not to do it, but he never listens, never!' and the other reached out, patted the thigh of the sniffly woman and said, 'I know!' Saskia got up and made herself a cup of coffee, studied the wrapped sandwiches in the little fridge and sat down again without taking one, but now with a couple of empty seats between her and the two women, whose repetitive dialogue continued at intervals. When Orson was finally brought back from his scan, she got up quickly and joined him in a cubicle again, sitting quietly on the chair in the corner. After a few minutes the same doctor as before turned up and after checking the stitches, she turned to Saskia.

'He has two skull fractures, at right angles, but only a very slight depression of the skull which is good – it's just where the fractures meet. There is minor brain swelling which might increase over the next twenty-four hours, so we'll move him to a ward upstairs and keep a close eye on him, but I don't think he needs to be in ICU. If we have to move him later we'll let you know.'

All the way up in the lift, into the ward, and then into a single room Saskia stayed right next to Orson, not touching him, just walking beside the bed. Suddenly she was exhausted, not sleepy, just very tired. It was now after three in the morning and the ward was quiet, the only sound was the hiss of rubber wheels on the vinyl floor. The room was nearly empty when they arrived, but within minutes equipment was wheeled in and placed beside the bed. A nurse hung two bags of colourless liquid on a stand and efficiently connected them via narrow tubes to an intriguing looking thing into a vein on the back of Orson's hand.

Saskia sat on the chair in the corner like a permanent fixture, silently watching and waiting. Next a male nurse came in with a monitor on a stand, connected it to Orson's arm and put a clip on his forefinger, and coloured lines and numbers appeared on the screen. Saskia added the monitor to her mental list of things to look up and learn about, but not right now with others in the room, perhaps later when she had showered and slept a few hours. That she was coming back in the morning was so obvious it didn't even enter her mind to consider it a choice, it was simply a fact.

The nurse turned to her and said, 'He'll probably just sleep once he comes out of this light coma, so why don't you go home and have a rest and come back in the morning?'

Not until Saskia was on the way home in a taxi did she realise that her phone was still muted and noticed missed call from Marian at twenty past one that morning. She had never had a call from Marian in the middle of the night and her first reaction was worry that something had happened, an accident perhaps or illness. Then she noticed a text alert and found a message from Marian sent at twenty-four minutes past one. *Will call tomorrow from work. Don't call back, I'll call you. M x*

If Saskia hadn't been so tired she wouldn't have been able to sleep after such a mysterious message, but exhaustion took over and she was asleep a few minutes after turning her bedside light off.

Chapter 12

When Saskia arrived at the hospital the next morning, equipped with all she would need to continue working, the door to the ward was closed, so she rang the bell on the wall and waited for a long while before someone came.

'Yes?' said the sturdy, middle-aged nurse, holding the edge of the door with one hand and looking out at Saskia, who stood there with her bag in her hand, hoping this was going to work. 'It's not visiting hours, I'm afraid.'

'I know,' Saskia said calmly and smiled her publicity smile. The one her publisher referred to as "the kind and innocent smile, the best possible contrast to the stuff you write".

'My cousin, Orson Dankworth was brought in during the night,' she continued. 'I came in with him and I'd like to sit with him for a while if that's possible. They said in the night that he might be confused when he wakes up and I want to be here to keep him calm. I promise I won't be in your way.'

The comment about confusion was invented on the spur of the moment, but to Saskia's surprise the nurse opened the door wider and stood back for Saskia to enter.

'He's not awake yet. I've just asked the doctor to come along and have a look at him. Do you remember the way to his room? I've got to get ready for the meds round, but I'll come and talk to you later.'

The room was silent and calm. Orson lay tidily on his back with tubes connected and the monitor lit up in yellow, red and green, a number occasionally changing or a line altering its course across the screen. Saskia went up to the bed on the far side where there was no equipment and dropped her bag on the floor.

'You poor man!' she said and put her hand on his, where it lay unmoving on the sheet. She curled her fingers around his, comforted by how warm his hand was, and reached behind her to pull the visitor's chair closer. She stayed like that until a doctor arrived half an hour later, a different doctor, male and younger than the one in the night.

'I'm doctor Faulkner - Josh,' he said. 'I gather you're Mr Dankworth's cousin? OK, he's still in a coma, not very deep – it sometimes happens after an impact like he had. The notes say you found him in the hallway by the lifts where you live. What was he like then?'

'Hi,' said Saskia and let go of Orson's hand. 'I'm Saskia. He was unconscious, lying on his back in a pool of blood and bleeding a lot. His legs were blocking the lift door and I think he'd probably only been there a few minutes before I heard the lift beeping and found him. I got a clean towel from my flat and made it into a pad to press against the wound, but he never moved apart from opening his eyes very briefly, just once, for maybe a couple of seconds.'

'Could you see how it happened, how he fell or what he hit his head on?'

She described the scene, how he had fallen sideways out of the lift and the mark she had noticed on the corner of the square column beside the lift door.

'Mm,' said Faulkner. 'It sounds as if he simply fell very heavily and hit the side of his head. He's hypotensive – he has low blood pressure - so perhaps his blood pressure dropped suddenly, but we'll never know. So, you don't suspect he was hit by anyone?'

'Oh, God no! The building is like Fort Knox, nobody could get in, and my neighbours are away. I'm sure it was just an accident.'

'That's what the ambulance crew thought as well,' he said, and looked closely at the monitor, as he spoke. 'They didn't report it as suspicious. I'll see you later.'

As soon as he left, Saskia opened the wardrobe in

the corner, and as she had expected, there were Orson's clothes, his jacket and trousers on hangers with a brown paper bag on the floor. In the bag she found a white shirt with a bloodstained collar, a pair of boxer shorts, socks and at the bottom, his shoes. Nice shoes, she thought, expensive, but the shirt is probably ruined. I'll have a go at that blood, but I bet it's too late now that it's dried. She left the shoes in the wardrobe and put the brown bag in the corner by the chair to take home when she left. After a few minutes a new idea popped up in her head, and she delved back into the bag, but there was no sign of a phone or a wallet. She opened the wardrobe again and checked the pockets in his jacket and trousers but found only a handkerchief and a folded a supermarket receipt.

Looking around the room she spotted the bedside cabinet on the far side of the bed with the monitor stand blocking it, and there in the drawer was his phone, wallet and keys. The phone lit up when she pressed the button on the side, but it was locked and there were no message alerts on the screen, so she returned it to the drawer and picket up the wallet.

Driver's licence, thirty-five dollars in cash, and a Southern Cross membership card. She put the wallet back and made a mental note about the card. That might come in useful, heaven knows what he might need at some stage. She sat down again and got her laptop out of her bag, plugged the charger in on the electrical panel on the wall behind the bed and put the bag on the floor. But seeing her phone and phone charger in the bag gave her an idea and she got Orson's phone out of the drawer again. Her charger cord fitted, so she plugged that in too.

'Just getting you organised, Orson - we might as well make sure it stays charged,' she said and put her hand on his shoulder, 'there's only thirty-eight percent in the battery and someone might call you or text. I'll check it for you at intervals and tell you what they say.'

When the nurse, who had let her in, arrived and found Saskia sitting on the upright chair with her laptop on top of the computer bag, all of it sloping perilously away from her on her knees, she said, 'That looks very uncomfortable! I'll see what I can find.'

She didn't come back for some time, but eventually she opened the door and said to someone in the corridor, 'You push the chair in first and then we'll take the table.' Within minutes Saskia had a small table and a wheeled typist's chair in the corner on the far side of the bed, the original upright chair was repositioned on the far side of the window, and two nurses watched with great satisfaction as Saskia put her laptop on the table.

'There!' said the older nurse. 'That's better! I love your books - I've read them all and I recognised you from the photo on the back covers. I thought you might want to write while you sit here, and now you can be comfortable.'

'That's so kind of you, Wendy,' said Saskia, who had read their name tags which only had first names. 'But I don't want preferential treatment. I'm sure you have far more important things to do. That's not one of the chairs from your office, I hope.'

'No, it's one of two from the two courtesy desk we have in the family room, I'll show you later.' They left accompanied by Saskia's repeated thanks.

For the next hour Saskia alternated between writing and watching Orson, and then she thought of something she had read, that some patients in a coma could hear what went on in the room, and some could even repeat what they head heard when they woke up much later. They said he's in a light coma, thought Saskia and wheeled her chair closer to Orson's bed, so let's try it.

'Hi, Orson,' she said in a normal voice, as if they were having a conversation. 'How are you feeling today?'

There was no movement, no flicker of an eyelid or any other sign that he had heard her, but she realised that talking to him was making her feel better, as if she were doing something constructive. And maybe she was, she thought, maybe he hears me though he can't show it, so he knows someone's here with him.

'I'll tell you something funny,' she continued and took his hand, which was warm and felt alive, but limp. 'On the way to the entrance from where I parked the car I met a guy who looked straight at me and when we were a few steps apart he said, "Do you know where Ladies Mile is?" and I started telling him it was a long way off and then I realised he was talking on his phone via ear buds. I felt like an idiot, Orson, and the way he looked at me! As if I should have known he was on the phone, but how could I? Don't you think that people who do that should have a little light on their forehead, like you have if you go camping in the dark? But instead of just a light it could say 'On air' like that light they have outside radio and TV studios.'

She let his hand drop back on the bed, looked at it and decided he would be more comfortable with it on his chest, picked it up again and put it on his lower ribcage. 'There you are,' she said and gave his hand a little pat. 'That looks better.'

Marian called at midday, and as soon as she had said "hi" Saskia knew something was terribly wrong.

'It's Tony, but I have to say this really fast, or I might burst into tears, and I've got to be back on the job in ten minutes.'

'That's OK.' Saskia was preparing herself to react appropriately for whatever was coming, but she couldn't hold back a gasp when Marian said bluntly. 'He's playing away.'

'Tony? Are you sure? Has he told you, admitted it?'

'I haven't asked, I can't bring myself to do it — what if he says he wants a divorce?'

'OK,' said Saskia slowly, thinking that she had heard about this. People who couldn't make themselves ask directly when they thought something was wrong, who would rather just torment themselves with worry than know for a fact. This was not a concept she would ever have imagined in relation to Marian, who was frank and open about most things. 'What makes you think he's — having an affair?'

'He's got this series of meetings on Wednesday nights, and it's been going on for four weeks now, but I don't believe it's meetings. I think he's having it off with someone. His secretary is young and *very* pretty ...'

'What does he say the meetings are about?'

Marian snorted, which in a way seemed like a good sign, a bit more like her usual down-to-earth persona. 'Supposedly planning meetings to do with a big merger his company is managing, you know how they get hired to be to facilitate when things get stuck during

negotiations.'

'Have you asked why they hold these meetings in the evenings?'

'Oh yes, that was the first thing I asked. He said some of the key people are hard to get together during the day, and they have offices quite far apart, so they've made it a regular time on a Wednesday evening. He said they don't want to do it on Zoom – they need to be in the same room. He goes to someone's office downtown and everyone meets there at half past six. Well – that's what he said. And then he comes home at nine or a bit after.'

Saskia wondered if she dared voice the question that had popped into her head, or if she should hang on to it for a later chat, perhaps from home, but she really felt she had hit on something.

'Have you ever had sex on a Wednesday since these meetings started?' she asked and tried to sound casual.

'Why are you … oh, I see,' said Marian and there was a longish silence at the other end before she said slowly, 'Wednesday last week we did. I remember because he came home and suggested we have a glass of wine and some cheese. He said he bought Chinese take-out food to eat before the meeting because he hadn't had time to have lunch, and it was so salty that he threw most of it a rubbish bin. And then we had another glass of wine and some more cheese and went to bed and …'

Yay! thought Saskia, and aloud she said, 'Well, it's just a thought, Marian, but do you think a man who's just come home from having sex with someone they're infatuated with, is likely to come home and have sex with his wife on the same night? Unless they're over-sexed and always at it like a randy rabbit.' Like Bruno, she thought, but Tony isn't a bit like him.

'You might be on to something there,' said Marian thoughtfully, not sounding totally convinced, but maybe she was thinking it could be proof of something positive. 'I'll check it next Wednesday, see if he's up to it.' Then she laughed briefly and added, 'I do know how to get him going, you know. He thinks he's sleepy or too tired or not in the mood, and I can have him raring to go in two minutes.'

'Are you going to share the trick?' asked Saskia out of mischief, just to see what Marion might say.

'No way! I might tell you most things, but not that one. Go learn your own tricks! Bye! Got to go.'

On the third day Saskia returned to the hospital at half past eight, grabbed a cup of coffee and some lunch from the café by the main entrance, a process which already felt like a routine, and stepped into the lift, thinking about a plotline that wasn't going where she had planned for it to go. That damn man! she thought about the main character's newly introduced best mate, he's developed a mind of his own, and now he's busy turning himself into someone quite different from the persona I had planned for him. Even at this late stage I might have to reconsider his character, or maybe I'll just kill him off, I'm fairly close to the end of the story now and maybe I could dispense with this irritating guy a bit early without ruining the plot.

Upstairs Orson lay in his quiet room just as she had left him late the night before, on his back with tubes going in and out and the monitors quietly ticking and winking. Today the head end of his bed had been raised slightly, and she liked how it made him seem less coma-like and more as if he had just closed his eyes to rest them.

'Hi, Orson!' she said and walked around the end of the bed to her little writing corner. 'How are you? I've just arrived. I washed my hair this morning and watered my plants, so all is well with the world. I'll just put my coffee and lunch on the table. I bought it from the café downstairs again, it's so handy. I'll tell you if it tastes as nice as it looks, but it looks delish - salmon and cream cheese on a bagel, one of my favourites.'

She bent down, held his shoulders with both hands and spoke close to his face. 'I hope you're OK in there, Orson, and that you can hear me. Would you please wake up soon, so I can make sure you're OK?'

She planted a kiss on his forehead and straightened up. There was, of course, no reply and no movement apart from his chest rising and falling. She knew she shouldn't have kissed him, but the impulse to give him some tangible affection overtook her common sense. She sighed at her own inexplicable behaviour, got her hairbrush out of her bag and brushed his hair, careful to avoid the dressing over the stiches, then stood back and looked critically at him. 'Sorry, Orson,' she said and wielded the brush again. 'I don't think that's how your hair wants to go. I'll do it this way instead. Ah, yes – that's much better.

Now you look like a tidy bear again, which is so nice seeing your name means bear-like. I thought it must have something to do with bears, so I looked it up.'

She sat down at her laptop and continued intermittently chatting about more or less meaningless things, wondering if inside his head he really could hear her voice and know someone was there with him, even if the words didn't register. Lying unmoving in a silent room, she thought, what a dreadful state to be in, and if he's even vaguely aware of things he'll not feel so lonely if he can hear a human voice. It will confirm he's still in the land of the living. I must Google this and see if it's true or just an urban myth.

'This is my new way of taking a five-minute break when I can't make up my mind about how to fix a tricky paragraph,' she told Orson two hours later, and took his hand in both hers. 'I'll sing you a song I really like, just slowly and quietly – it's one Dolly Parton wrote and if you sing it slowly it's like a lullaby.'

At home she would open the solitaire app and play a couple of games on her laptop, when she was having break or needed to think of the next stage of the story, and then go back to writing. Here, she either went for a walk along the corridor to the visitors' bathroom or she talked, read or sang to Orson. Already she had established a set of little routine breaks in the day, things she did mid-morning, straight after lunch and late afternoon. The nurses had started giving her a coffee whenever they made one for themselves, and twice a day she got down on the floor and did ten push-ups and then ten sit-ups with her hands clasped behind her neck.

'Isn't I marvellous they let me come in before visiting time every day, so I can keep you company? But I don't understand why I can't use the bathroom attached to this room,' she said to him now when she had finished the song. 'It's not as if you're going to use it to pee or have a shower, is it? I'm sure you wouldn't mind if I used it. But I won't do it, I promise. I'm here on sufferance, so I've got to behave.'

She put Orson's hand back on his bare chest, gave it a little pat and straightened the sheet across his midriff before she went back to her writing.

'I want to hire you for a private job,' said Saskia to the middle-aged and heavily tattooed man in the barber's shop just around the corner and down the block from her apartment the next morning. It was early and she knocked on the door to get him to open. 'I know you're not open yet, but I saw you through the window, and this is the only time I can talk to you face to face. What's your name?'

'Henry,' he said, looking slightly suspicious. 'What kind of job?'

'Oh, nothing irregular, don't worry!' Saskia laughed at his frown. What did he think? That she wanted to hire him to murder someone? 'I've got a cousin who's unconscious in hospital after a fall, and his stubble's growing very fast and soon it will be a thick black beard and he'll look like a dangerous pirate. I'd like someone to come along twice a week and shave him, or maybe three times would be better, if that's possible. I'll pay for it, including taxis. You can charge me however you like. An hourly fee, probably as it will take time to go there and back? I can pay you by coming in here and using my card once a week, or you can just tell me how much it is at intervals, and I can pay cash.'

'Where is he? What happened to him?'

'I don't know what happened. I found him lying half in and half out of the lift in the middle of the night – we're in next-door apartments. Maybe he tripped, or he might have collapsed because he has very low blood pressure. He hit his head very hard on the concrete pillar just beside the lift. He cracked his skull, and he had a terrible cut on his scalp, bled like a pig. Can you do it?'

'OK,' said Henry. 'I can come along after five, probably six by the time I close here. We'll see how we go - it might be easier to do it every second day if his beard grows fast. But you'll have to clear it with the staff at the hospital, and you'll have to tell me which ward he's in and what his name is.' He thought for a moment. 'It would probably be best if you're there, too. I mean, what if he wakes up and panics? I'll be holding a cut-throat razor after all – I presume you want it done properly?'

They loaded each other's numbers on their phones, and Saskia left feeling that she had achieved something good, a practical thing and maybe not necessary, but restoring Orson's face to how it normally looked seemed like a positive thing to do.

Chapter 14

On day eight, right after Saskia had finished her daily sit-ups and got up from floor, panting slightly, she got a text from Marian. She had been thinking of Marian every day since that inconclusive talk they had several days ago. A couple of times she had nearly called her, but somehow it seemed too intrusive, so she decided to wait for Marian to call her.

'It worked again,' said Marian without any greeting and sounded reasonably cheerful. 'He came home at quarter to ten last night and said he'd had a shitty day dealing with totally unreasonable people and the meeting had taken longer than it should and how about we opened the bottle of bubbly that had been sitting in the fridge for a fortnight.'

'And?' said Saskia, who could hear Tony's voice in her head, saying that. She knew him so well she could even imagine the intonation, the stress he would put on *totally*. 'Then you ...'

'We did,' said Marian, 'with a vengeance, like he was making up for his shitty day. So maybe those meetings really are work, not him having it off with his secretary.'

The door opened and Josh, the friendly doctor came in, so Saskia said a quick goodbye and put her phone down.

'Hi there,' said Josh. 'The nurses tell me there's been no sign of life, sorry! I didn't mean to say that - such a standard phrase, but not the right one here. I mean, he's not moved or reacted to anything?'

Saskia found herself putting a protective hand on Orson's as if he might feel upset about having been referred to as showing no signs of life. 'No, nothing so far, no movement and he's not opened his eyes. But I'm sure he can hear me talking to him.'

'Really? So, he's changed in some way?'

'No, but I know,' said Saskia firmly, looking straight at the doctor across Orson's bed. 'I can feel it when I talk to him or read to him, it's like ... well, I don't know how to describe it, but I'm quite sure.'

She could see he didn't believe her. He thought she was indulging in comforting, wishful thinking and if there were no signs of Orson waking up he would discount what she said. She read his face and changed the subject.

'Have you had patients like him before - people

who were in a light coma for this length of time? Or is it no longer regarded as a light coma?'

'I haven't personally come across it, but it does happen. One day, hopefully soon, he'll just open his eyes and say hi. And we're stopping the antibiotics tonight seeing there's no sign of infection in the wound and it's healing well. We'll have the stitches out later today.'

On his way out of the room he turned and said, 'He looks very tidy. Who shaves him? Do you do it?'

Saskia laughed. 'I wouldn't have any idea how to do it properly, not on someone like Orson, who grows hair like the bear he's named after. I've organised for a proper barber to come in every second day, and he does it with an old-fashioned cut-throat razor.'

'Wow – what devotion!' said Josh and left.

'Don't pay any attention to him, Orson,' she said when the door had shut behind him. 'Just ignore him – he doesn't know as much as he thinks he does. I *know* you can hear me.'

The days rolled past, and nothing changed. Saskia continued to arrive at half past eight every morning, and apart from going down to the café once or twice every day to buy something to eat, she didn't leave until eight or later. Staff no longer checked Orson's room when visiting time was over and she would just quietly let herself out when she felt it was time to go home. She left her laptop in Orson's wardrobe and only carried a shoulder bag with her phone, her keys and her small backup device. Now her apartment seemed like a temporary place when she got home, just somewhere to run some clothes through the washing machine and sleep.

To feel lonely in her own apartment didn't strike her as strange; she knew the reason and despite talking to friends on the phone some evenings or watching a movie, just as she used to before the Orson incident, it wasn't the same; she felt as if something was missing. Her real existence was in Orson's room at the hospital, however strange that seemed when she really thought about it, but she couldn't shake the feeling off and just carried on. She sometimes looked at their shared apartment wall and wondered if there were pot plants dying of thirst in there, milk curdling in the fridge or something he'd taken out of the freezer to thaw out, slowly rotting on his kitchen bench. She could have taken his keys and gone in to check things were all right, but it was a step too far, an intrusion into his privacy that she couldn't quite bring herself to make.

On day thirteen Marian called and invited Saskia to Sunday lunch. 'Sorry, I would have loved to,' said Saskia. 'I haven't seen you for ages, but I'm busy this weekend, both days. Let's make it next weekend or the one after. I might have to knuckle down and get that damn book finished before I have a social life again.'

She didn't dare ask about Tony and whether Marian was now comfortable the Wednesday meetings were genuine. Last time she mentioned it Marian had seemed reasonably confident, but she hadn't said anything since. They ended the call with a promise to be in touch soon and Saskia sat looking at Orson, whose head seemed to be slightly turned to one side. Had he been like that all morning? She got up and went to stand at the end of his bed, where she paused every morning to say hi to him, on her way to her little corner on the far side of the bed.

'I'm not sure, Orson,' she said now. 'I think I would have noticed.'

Behind her Wendy, the nurse who seemed to be in charge most days, said, 'Anything wrong?'

Saskia turned and shook her head. 'I might be imagining things, just wishful thinking, but I can' remember Orson's head being turned slightly to the side like that when I got here this morning.'

They stood side by side and studied Orson, then Wendy said, 'You might be right. We usually straighten him out when we've turned him, if we do it in the morning, but the night staff did it at five am today, so I can't really say. Keep an eye on him for me, will you, and ring the bell if he moves. I'm coming back with a new bag a saline a bit later on, I'll see you then.'

For the first time Saskia took a photo of Orson from the foot end of the bed, lining herself up to be dead centre, but by the time she left that evening, nothing had changed.

On day fourteen she took another photo as soon as she arrived, and when she came back from buying her lunch in the café, Orson's head was turned to the left again, but a bit more this time. She rang the bell and stood watching him like a hawk until a nurse arrived.

'Look!' she said. 'See the way his head's turned to the left and then look at this photo which I took at eight thirty-five this morning.'

She held her phone out and they both looked at the photo, then at Orson and then back again. 'Great!' said the nurse and went to the side of the bed. 'Let's see if there's a bit of response.' She lifted Orson's arm, bent it and let it drop.

'A little bit of resistance there,' she said cheerfully. 'I'll go and make a note of it. Tell me if anything else happens, but I think he's on the way to waking up. I'll get a doctor to do some proper reflex tests later, if I can get hold of one of them.'

I'm so lucky, thought Saskia, when the nurse had left. Sitting in her corner she contemplated the routine, which had evolved over the last fortnight, and the exceptions and allowances that had been made for her. Each morning when she arrived at the ward they let her in and greeted her as if she were part of the team. When she got to Orson's room she would run a wet facecloth over his face while she chatted to him, because early on she had tried to imagine what she herself would appreciate most if she were in his place and being gently wiped with cool water had instantly come to mind. Then she brushed his hair and checked everything around him to see if anything had changed, and studied the data displayed on the monitor, all of which she could now decipher, then she checked the bags on the IV stand. Over the past two weeks she had looked up and read on the internet about everything related to his care and sometimes checked things further with the doctor or the nurses. Orson was only tethered to a bag of saline now, a bag of the liquid nutrition mixture that went through a tube into a vein in his groin and a urine catheter.

'Really? Food via the groin?' she said to a nurse at an early stage. 'How bizarre!' And the nurse told her about the best veins to feed it into for patients in a coma, and how they didn't always use the same vein and why. The scar on the side of his head was rapidly disappearing into thick black hair, and not for the first time she marvelled at the way his beard and hair grew. Thank goodness Henry comes every second day, she thought, or Orson really would look like the swarthy captain of a pirate ship by now.

Chapter 15

The next morning, she took another photo of Orson's position in the bed and wondered why he still lay here in coma such a long time after she had opened her door and found him lying in a pool of blood. Today his head was perfectly straight, and she knew she would notice if it changed even by a fraction. She glanced at the checklist that hung on the rail at the end of Orson's bed and saw he had been turned on his side twice in the night.

'It's all good, Orson,' said Saskia now and put her hand lightly on his bare chest. 'I don't know *how* they do it at night when they've only got minimal staff on. It takes two strong nurses to roll you over, you know, and that little shrimp of a girl who was on yesterday afternoon, she'd be no help at all. But we don't want you to get pneumonia or pressure sores, so it's got to be done. I see they've tilted your bed up a tiny bit more today – you're nearly halfway to sitting up. Is it nice?'

When they moved him in the daytime or in the early evening, she often helped by holding tubes and wires safely out of the way, but at night two nurses had to cope on their own, though she smiled at the thought that they would need her assistance. During any process of Orson being moved she would watch and wonder why he seemed to be so heavy. He was a big man, but he seemed to weigh a ton, far more than she would have expected. Or did he just seem heavy because he was limp and couldn't help by holding his body steady? It wasn't that he was overweight, he was tall and broad, so perhaps it was just that he had a lot of mass.

'Like a black hole,' she said now and ran her hand over his cheek. 'You're like a black hole, Orson - dense mass and therefore very, very heavy. No insult intended, just a friendly observation.'

Orson didn't move or speak, just lay silent and still with only his chest moving and Saskia sighed.

It was a bit early to call anyone at work, way before their morning break, she imagined, but she might chat to Matthew for a few minutes before his day got busy. She had been focused on Orson for so long now, trying to get on with her writing at the same time. A few times she had talked to friends who had called and today she wanted to hear another voice than her own. She had no idea if other writers called their agent just to have a chat, but since Matthew had been her agent she talked to him quite often. They got on well right from the start and she found him amusing; his conventional way of looking at things, and the way he got a bit flustered when she teased him was irresistible. He's a bit like someone's granddad, thought Saskia and smiled at the thought, not like a guy in his thirties.

'Are you completely insane?' asked Matthew five minutes later. 'Having a barber come in and shave him while he's lying there like a slab of meat? I mean, even if he is *vaguely* a friend, whatever that means, it's a bit crazy even for you.'

'Don't be an idiot, Matthew,' said Saskia cheerfully and took a sip of the cooling mug of coffee a nurse had brought in. 'I want him to look nice, like he does in normal life. He's a nice-looking beast, and this damn black beard he was growing made him look like a pirate or something in no time at all. Hang on, I'll – oh, no, I won't.'

'You won't what? What *are* you talking about now?'

'I was going to show you the pirate look, it's very stubbly just now, he's getting a shave tonight, but I think that would be a bit off, like invading his privacy, so I won't.'

'Are you at the hospital *now*? At this time of the

morning? How come you're there when it's not visiting time?'

'Oh, I'm here all the time, or nearly all the time. I come in quite early in the morning and go home at night. They've set up a nice little writing corner for me in his room with a comfortable table and a chair, so I can continue writing. Now and then I stop and read a passage out to Orson, or I just chat to him, so he won't feel so lonely. It's a bit over two weeks since the accident and he hasn't had a single visitor.'

'You really are quite mad, but very lovely,' said Matthew. 'I never know what to expect next. So, can he hear you talking?'

'Nobody knows what or if he can hear. I sing to him quite a lot, just quiet, slow songs in case he's having a snooze in there, inside his head. The doctor who's in charge of him says it's very possible that he can hear despite being in a coma. Apparently it's not a deep coma and sometimes patients wake up and can tell staff what they heard, so I've got to be careful not to say anything rude.' She laughed. 'I'm sure I've shocked him once or twice. But I've read up on it and it's important for him to have stimulation, not just music or radio or something monotonous – if he *can* hear. He might be listening to me talking to you right now. Do you want to say hello to him?'

'No thank you! And how's the book coming along? Did you solve the problem with your recalcitrant character'

'You know such wonderful words, Matthew! Well, lots of people do, but you *use* them. I only ever use words like that when I write. Yes, I've let the hero's best mate become the person he always wanted to be instead of killing him off. It's meant doing quite a bit of editing to tidy his persona up, but it's ok now and he's doing fine. It's probably an improvement, actually. The girl he's after is a bit of a drip, so I think I'll have to make her argumentative and feisty, she's not in his class at all. Give him some excitement before the end of the book.'

She laughed quietly thinking of the rather timid girl she had given him. 'He'll probably get bored with her after a couple of months and walk all over her if I don't change her a bit. I might make them have a fight, I think – perhaps at night, in the rain and for her to just walk away. Make him think. Or she could take his pistol out of the back of his belt and walk off with it – that might be good, and he tries to take it back and it goes off. God, Matthew, I'd better stop talking I've got a whole chapter in my head now that I've got to insert in the right place, drama and trauma – great!'

'You always talk about them as if they are real,' said Matthew in a slightly disbelieving voice.

'They *are* real!' she said, deeply indignant that someone who lived and worked in the world of books was such an ignoramus. 'Of course, they are! To me they're as real as you are – no, they're *more* real than you because they're part of my daily life. Once I get to roughly six thousand words, they take on a life of their own. They develop characteristics I never knew they had and say things I never planned for them to say. This guy I've been having problems with - yesterday he said something so out of character I had to go back and change a few things I'd written about him *again*. I could tell he wasn't going to change, the stubborn bastard.'

She rolled her wheeled chair a bit closer to the bed and took hold of Orson's hand the way she often did. Human touch, she thought, and curled her fingers around his and stroked his knuckles with her thumb, such an important sensation, and if I wasn't here he'd not get enough of it, hardly any.

'Yesterday afternoon my hero described to a thug exactly how he was going to break his elbow, as a threat,' she continued telling Matthew. 'I'll tell you how to do it in case you ever need to do it to someone. I don't think I'm strong enough to do it, but I could stand by and instruct you. First you bend their arm at right angles at the elbow and then you anchor the upper arm to the side of the ribcage and bend the lower arm hard backwards, a really hard and fast swivel - it's excruciatingly painful apparently. I asked a doctor I met in the café downstairs what I could use, something really nasty that didn't need weapons, just hands, and she said break his elbow and told me how to do it. We had a lovely conversation about all the possible ways she could think of to harm people with your bare hands - not just the usual things everybody uses like punches and kicks to the groin or whatever. I've got her number now, so I can call her when I need help. This place is full of useful people.'

'Well, that's a positive thing to take from this crazy venture of yours,' said Matthew and she could hear he was smiling. 'Get as much info as you can while you have the chance.'

When she finished talking to Matthew she sat for a long while, still holding Orson's hand, and read out bits of what she had written since she last filled him in. As always, Orson lay still, breathing quietly, then suddenly his hand twitched in hers. His fingers gripped her hand and held on tight for more than just a second, maybe ten seconds or longer, she couldn't tell, she was so excited she could hardly breathe. Then his grip slackened, and he turned his head in her direction and opened his eyes. She saw his gaze focus on her, he blinked twice and closed them again. He sighed and lay still, his head still turned towards her.

'Oh, Orson! You moved!' she cried, and with tears pooling in her eyes she bent forward and impulsively put her cheek against his for a moment. 'Are you awake? Are you OK?'

But Orson didn't reply, and his hand was slack once again. Still holding it in hers, Saskia wiped her eyes with the back of her free hand and rang the bell.

'You won't believe it!' she said excitedly when the

nurse came in. 'He heard me reading to him, he did! I was holding his hand and he gripped my hand really tight, and he opened his eyes!'

Doctor Faulkner came in with a nurse, glanced at Orson and said, 'Was he conscious, eyes open? Did he speak?'

'Oh, yes – he was definitely conscious,' said Saskia. 'I was reading to him, holding his hand, and he gripped my hand hard and held on tight. Not just a quick reflex or whatever you'd call it, it was deliberate, he held on really hard. He didn't say anything, but I saw his eyes focus on me, I could tell he was seeing me.'

The various checks took ages, while Saskia fretted about not being able to talk to Orson to see if she could get him to say something. They tested his reflexes, shone a light into his eyes and tried to get him to grip their hands, then Faulkner said, 'He's waking up, there's definite more muscle response there. Ring the bell if he does.' And then he was off to see patients who needed him more urgently.

About an hour later, when Saskia had just returned from the visitors' restroom down the corridor, Orson opened his eyes again and looked first up at the ceiling and then straight at her when she made a sound of surprise.

'Where am I - who are you?' he asked, his voice hoarse and weak at the same time. 'What happened?'

Thank God there aren't any nurses to hear this! thought Saskia and smiled at Orson. Aloud she said, 'I'm Saskia, I'm … I'm here visiting, we've met once or twice.'

Suddenly the idea of telling him the details, that they were neighbours and that she was the one who had found him was an impossible task. Even without thinking about it she knew that too much information at this stage might overwhelm him. And suddenly she remembered the one time she had shared the lift with him, and it was like experiencing a dislocation in time, it jolted her to think of it. She couldn't possibly picture herself reaching out for the hand of the man who had stood beside her, silent and solid, from the ground floor to level three. Or stroking his wrist. And as for running her fingers over his stubbly cheek while humming a tune to keep him entertained! The image in her mind made her cringe, and she wondered how she could have done all those things to the unconscious body of a stranger and feel they were connected. Maybe I am going mad, she thought, maybe I've lost my mind already and nobody's told me.

It was clear from his expression that what she had said meant nothing to him. 'Saskia?' he said as if he was tasting the name. 'Saskia – no, I don't remember.'

'Don't worry about it,' she said quickly. 'Your

accident might have made you forget things. You'll remember everything by and by, I'm sure. The important thing is that I've lied to the staff here and said I'm your cousin, and it would be really good if you could back me up. If you don't mind. Can you remember that? I told them I'm your cousin, so I could come and visit you.'

His eyes moved around the room, followed the tube from his hand up to the IV stand beside the bed, to the monitor and then back to Saskia. 'OK, I'll remember, you're my cousin. But what happened, why am I here?'

'You fell and hit your head and fractured your skull.'

She got up and walked around the bed and took his hand, which now had the normal slight resistance of consciousness, and carefully watched the IV-line bending, making sure it didn't snag. 'Here,' she said and moved his fingertips over the scar. 'Feel that? You had fourteen stiches, but they've come out now.'

He closed his eyes, his forehead creased, and he said slowly, 'Stitches – and they've come out? How long have I been here?' Aha, thought Saskia, his mind is working, he figured out the time gap straight away, very good!

'Fifteen days, I think. But *please* try to remember I'm your cousin. That's what I had to say, or they would never have let me, ah, visit you.'

He nodded without opening his eyes, and then suddenly he was asleep, she could tell from his breathing and how his hand felt in hers. Not back in the coma state, just sleeping. Now that he seemed to be all right, Saskia decided to leave earlier than she usually did. Thinking ahead to the conversation she must have with him next time he woke up made her feel very worried and insecure. She needed to think about it before he woke up again, and she must have some reasonable explanations ready, so she didn't sound completely crazy.

She stopped at the nurses' office and said, 'Sorry, I've just had message about a minor family emergency, so I have to leave early. I hope to be back at my normal time tomorrow. Oh, and Orson woke up again and we had a short conversation, then he fell asleep. And he's sleeping now, not in a coma, just sleeping.'

'Did he sound coherent? Fully aware?'

'Oh, yes – we had a little chat, and when I told him he had had fourteen stitches, but they had come out a few days ago, he straight away worked out he must have been unconscious for quite a while. It didn't sound as if anything is wrong with his mind.'

All the way home she debated with herself and wondered if there really was some way of justifying what she had done and why. How would she tell Ross about this, for example? Not that she was planning to, but if she decided to tell him, how would she put it?

In her head she constructed a dialogue to see where it would go.

'Dad, my neighbour fell over by the lift and split his head open in the middle of the night, and I found him, so I went with him in the ambulance and sat in ED for hours.'

And Ross would say, 'Why one earth did you do that? I didn't know he was a friend of yours.' He'd have that slightly puzzled expression he sometimes displayed when she strayed into her imagined world.

'He was so lonely,' she'd say, 'and I didn't want him to feel worried when he woke up.'

And Ross would probably say, 'How do you know he'd be lonely? How well do you know him?'

'Oh, I don't know him at all, I just knew when I touched him that he was very alone.' And her father would look hard at her and say, 'Saskia, I think you've written yourself into one of your stories! You'll have to extricate yourself smartly before this becomes a real mess. You've invaded his privacy and falsified a hospital document! What were you thinking?'

That night sleep took a long time coming, but while she lay there with repetitive thoughts revolving in her mind she gradually arrived at what she felt was a reasonable way of easing away from embarrassment and possible blame. Not a perfect solution, but something Orson might accept, so he would understand why it was better not to tell the staff at the hospital that she wasn't really his cousin. Her dreams were fragmented, and she woke a couple of times, drank some water and managed to get back to sleep, but she slept lightly, disturbed by uneasy dreams.

Chapter 16

The following morning an orderly leaving the ward held the door open so Saskia could enter. The ward seemed very quiet, and she saw nobody as she walked down the hallway, but she stopped abruptly just before she got to the door to Orson's room when a sudden insight struck her like a blow on the head. She couldn't see him, not even briefly, not now and probably never again. Last night when she had sat up late in the nearly dark living room, looking out over the harbour trying to make up her mind how this would work out, and later in bed, she felt she had solved the problem. How she would present her case, as she thought of it, to avoid upsetting him or making him angry, and how to avoid the staff at the hospital becoming furious with her. And then she had still come here this morning without the details worked out, as if some solution would magically present itself and make what she said credible and acceptable. But now in an instant she knew she was wrong to hope for a soft landing. It simply wasn't going to happen, and she must reconsider before it was too late to turn back.

The feeling of strong connection that had arisen from her urge to protect him and help him had no validity in reality, it was all in her head. It was a purely one-sided experience and none of it was real, because only she knew it and felt it. He had no idea of what had gone on all that time, and to him she was a stranger, not part of his life.

I have no right to be here, she thought and swallowed hard to avoid a sob escaping. I'm nothing to him, just a fleeting by-stander with no right to lasting involvement. Just some mysterious stranger he talked to briefly when he first woke up. God, I shouldn't have come back here today, this could turn into a nightmare, it was a stupid thing to do.

She stood there in the corridor and quickly considered her options. The best plan would be to wait until they showered him, as they had said they would do this morning when she stopped by the nurses' office yesterday when she was leaving. She felt certain they wouldn't let him shower on his own in case he fell, not after being flat on his back for so long and having low blood pressure, so a nurse or two would be in the bathroom with him, and first thing in the morning they would have been too busy to do it.

When they were in the bathroom would be the perfect opportunity to enter his room, quickly remove her belongings and quietly disappear.

Retreating to the little bay further down the corridor from Orson's room, from where she could see his door by leaning slightly sideways, she sat battling a devastating feeling of loss. Processing this would be hard and she felt bereft already, but she must do it. It seemed incredible to her now that this had not occurred to her earlier, that she had continued to be here, to hold his hand and tell him things and never once seriously considered what it would be like when he woke up. Or maybe in the back of her mind she had known it, but right from the start that strong feeling that she must protect him had pushed all other considerations aside. More than two weeks of daily interactions, if you could call it that, with a man who was an unconscious stranger, had given her a false sense of connection, and now she must somehow apply reason and make herself regard him as a stranger again. But how could she? She felt intense sadness at the thought, but it had to happen.

Matthew knew, she thought, he got it straight away, but he didn't say it and I was in my own little world where everything I did was for the best of reasons, so I just ignored his concern. And he was concerned, even though he didn't know I wasn't even a vague friend of Orson's, like I told him I was. What would he have said if I'd told him the truth, that

Orson is a total stranger, and I was impersonating a cousin?

Her phone played the little four-note tune that signalled an incoming message and she fished it out of her bag.

From Henry: 'Orson awake when I arrived last night. You had already left, he didn't know I'd been coming, said I'm not needed now.'

From Saskia: 'I'm sorry, should have warned you (and him). Will come in and pay final bill this morning.'

Half an hour later a nurse entered Orson's room with two towels and a pair of blue hospital PJs over his arm, and Saskia got up and approached slowly. She could hear them talking, the nurse's voice slightly lighter and Orson's darker, and then after a few minutes the shower in his bathroom was turned on. What a lucky thing it shares a wall with the corridor, thought Saskia and listened intently. Something scraped across the floor in there and she could hear the nurse chatting away. Good! There were both in the bathroom now. She went in, pulled the door nearly shut behind her and rapidly threw her things into her laptop case, cast a final glance around to check nothing was left and left.

She looked back to the recessed seating area at the coffee mug and bag of lunch she had left on one of the chairs. Let someone else get a surprise lunch, she thought, but after a few steps she turned back, fished her pen out of her bag and wrote on the paper bag, 'Orson, I'm so sorry but I have to leave right away and you're in the shower. Family emergency. See you soon, S.' She put the mug and the bag on the floor just inside his door and left without looking back.

Chapter 17

After considering the questions Henry might ask and how she should respond, she had still reached no conclusion when she entered the barber's shop feeling unsettled and apprehensive. The feeling increased until it was nearly unbearable as she sat unseeingly looking at a magazine as he finished shaving an elderly man and then cut the hair of another.

'Nice guy – it was good to be able to have a chat with him,' said Henry when his customers had paid and left together. 'He was still a bit muddled last night, but what can you expect? He's been out of it for so long.'

In Saskia's mind a further string of consequences, in addition to those she had already tried to predict, unrolled like a long fuse leading to a bomb she couldn't see.

'What did he say?' she asked hoping she didn't sound anxious. 'Was he rude?'

Henry laughed and she realised that not only was he covered in tattoos, but he had a stud through his tongue as well. 'No, no, he wasn't rude, he was just surprised. When I walked in he asked who I was, which I kind of expected, of course. When I got there a nurse told me he'd woken up and that you'd had to leave early, and I thought you mightn't have had time to explain about me. So, I said I'd been coming every two or three days and he thought the hospital had organised it.'

He laughed again, hugely enjoying playing the scene back for Saskia's benefit. 'I told him you'd organised it, and he said he didn't have a cousin in town, he looked really confused. But he let me shave him, and you know how you said to talk to him when he was unconscious - I just carried on as usual, and I said your cousin told me she didn't like you with a beard because it made you look like a pirate.'

'What did he say to that?' asked Saskia and wished she had been a fly on the wall during the shaving episode, which sounded like something she could have written in a book. 'Did he mind?'

'No, not at all, he laughed, but then he got a bit confused again and said yes, he did have a couple of cousins, and asked if I knew your name, so I said your name was Saskia, and he said, yes, of course, it was

Saskia – he was so relieved that he'd remembered. But he was very grateful at the end and said he'd never been shaved by anyone with a real razor before and how good it felt after. Who cuts your hair?'

For a moment Saskia was the one who was confused and thought he was still quoting from his chat with Orson, and then she realised he was looking critically at her hair.

'A place downtown, in High Street, I've been going there forever. Why, don't you approve?'

'No, I don't,' he said bluntly, and taking her by one shoulder he turned her around and lifted her thick hair up from her neck. 'Waste of time going there, this isn't any good on you. Didn't they ever suggest anything else?' He ran his fingers through her hair over the contours of her skull. 'Your head is a very pretty shape, and all this hair just hides it. And it's too thick and heavy, it weighs you down.'

She glanced at their reflection in the mirror, with Henry beside her holding her hair up with one hand and the other still clasping her skull under the hair and didn't know what to think. She studied her familiar face (oval), her dead-straight eyebrows (dark brown), her short nose and slightly longer than shoulder length medium-blond hair, very thick and as always vaguely wavy towards the ends. 'What's wrong with it? Are you a ladies' hairdresser as well?'

'Yep, trained as both.' Henry met her gaze in the

mirror. 'Please let me cut your hair – this is all wrong for the shape of your head and your face. And we should do some foils, highlights would work wonders with this thick hair all the same colour. How old are you?'

'Nearly thirty-nine.' She started to laugh. 'What's this inquisition in aid of, Henry?'

'Give me a couple of hours and I'll make you ten years younger - at least.' She stared at him, and he looked back, deadly serious. 'I'm not joking, I can see exactly what you *could* look like, just gorgeous. You've got fabulous skin and no wrinkles, and what could go wrong? What's your job?'

'I'm an author – crime fiction.'

'So, you work from home, then? Pity! After I've finished with you, you'd knock their socks off if you walked back into an office tomorrow - they wouldn't recognise you, I guarantee it.'

This morning is full of shocks and surprises, thought Saskia and only took one moment to decide to let Henry do whatever he wanted. Today was already a sad and confusing day, so why not let him do whatever he had in mind. What did it matter? It wasn't as if she had to go anywhere and if it was awful she could put her pink cap on when she went out, that would hide the worst. She wanted to change herself into someone else, a woman who didn't feel the deep sadness that still crouched inside her, behind the light-hearted exchange with Henry.

'OK,' she said, 'you can do it, but promise you won't dye it red or black. Why haven't you got any other clients today?'

'This isn't really a barber's shop.' He lowered his voice and glanced at the door, nearly whispered. 'It's just a front, I only have a few clients, I run a drug business from here.' Then he laughed his huge laugh again. 'Take that look off your face, Miss Crime-writer! I can see the cogs moving in your head. I'm never open on a Monday, I have Sunday and Monday off, but I came down to do a stocktake to see what needs ordering, and then those two old gents, who always come in together, called and I said they could come in. And just so you know, I really do have a clientele of women as well as men. I do know what I'm doing.'

The slow transformation that followed was scary and exciting at the same time. First he cut her hair off to a couple of centimetres below her earlobes, which made her neck feel cold and her head feel light. Perhaps she had got so used to the weight of her hair pulling her head back and compensated for it, she thought, that now it nearly tipped forward without anything to anchor it at the back. Then he parted it into thin strands, painted on whatever colour it was he had decided on and folded foil around each one.

'What colour is that white foamy stuff going to be?' asked Saskia suspiciously half-way through the process. 'It's not going to turn red, is it? You promised!'

'It's not red and it's not black. Don't worry, I know what I'm doing,' he said again and smiled at her worried face in the mirror.

'Yeah, right! The last person who said that blew both his hands off while making a home-made bomb.'

'Really? I didn't hear about that – when was this?' He was instantly interested, eyes gleaming with curiosity.

She had to think, was it two or three years ago? 'I think it was three years ago,' she said slowly. 'Yes, it was! In a book called Don't Look Now. It's about an amateur terrorist, not very competent, who ultimately ends up dead as a doornail. Great fun.'

'Aha!' He grinned at her reflection. 'You wrote a *book* with this guy in it. Why was it fun – do you mean it was fun to write?'

'The research was great fun. I love science, and writing the kind of books that I write, I need to find out lots of stuff. My Google history is probably monitored by the security services all over the globe like I'm a would-be terrorist or something. Getting tech and factual things right is important, though every now and then some little thing has to be tweaked a bit out of true to fit the story. Bomb making was taking it a bit far and when my agent heard what I was planning he got me a live source instead of me searching the internet and getting into trouble.'

'Like a real person? Someone who knows about bombs, like a terrorist?'

'No, of course not! An army guy who knew everything there is to know, he's in the bomb squad, a very serious guy. He had absolutely no imagination at all – which probably explains how he could be in a job like that. He gave me all the info I needed, but he insisted I made the description wrong in a vital detail, so my book couldn't be used as a blueprint for bomb making.' She laughed at the memory. 'And then when I'd made lots of notes and we were parting, I said it's so good to know which bit is wrong, and what it should be, in case I ever need to make a bomb. He looked quite worried when he left.'

Finally, the foils were done, and her head looked like a shiny porcupine. Henry set a timer and said, 'Coffee or tea? It's nearly lunchtime and I need one. I went out and bought chicken sandwiches this morning, we can share those.'

After sharing Henry's sandwiches and a large chocolate and hazelnut bar from Saskia's bag, he was ready to finish the job. Her hair was washed, then cut again with greater precision, and then Henry said, 'Now that we've finetuned the cut, here's the final act – blow-drying this style the right way. Keep your eyes open now, so you learn how to do it yourself, it's important to know where to start.'

And right before her eyes, the shortish, wet hair transformed into a pageboy bob with blond highlights in amongst her own colour, and snap! there was a stranger looking back at her, a woman she had never seen before. A younger woman than the one who had come in a couple of hours ago, with a pointy chin and big eyes and a fringe right across her forehead, half a centimetre above her eyebrows.

Saskia silently stared at her image in the mirror for so long that Henry got worried. 'Don't you like it? Too different?'

'Oh God, no! I love it - you're a wizard, Henry! I had no idea I could look like this. And I didn't know my face was this pointy shape – how extraordinary.'

'You look amazing,' said Henry proudly and held up a mirror to show her from the back and the side. 'Have you got a brush like this?'

He showed her a cylindrical brush, and she shook her head. 'I have a drier of course, but not that kind of brush. Can you sell me one?'

'Of course, and if you need help with the blow-drying at any time, just pop in and I'll do it for you on the spot. Where do you live?'

'Just down the street and around the corner in that block of flats with the black detail. The one someone called the chess board building in an article when it was new.'

'Lucky you! I suppose you're on the side with a view of the sea?'

'I am, and it *is* lovely, but mine is just a smallish flat in the middle of the front. There are two huge flats each side that go right around the corners with balconies both sides. For people with lots and lots of money.'

When she paid for Orson's last three shaves and her own haircut, it was three hours after she had arrived, and her mood had changed a little.

I can overcome this, she told herself as she walked home. I'm a different person now - I look and feel different, and Henry's a fun new friend. I'm a survivor, and I'll not let sadness dominate my life. This is what I'll tell myself every day until I this feeling of loss and grief fades into the past.

It wasn't until she got home that the further consequences of the whole Orson episode struck her, and she stopped with her hand on the tap to fill a glass of water. There were loose ends, she realised, things that couldn't be left dangling. She sat down with her shopping pad and made some notes, drank some water, then got up and walked around while she tried to work out the best way of doing this, sat down again, drank some more water, made more notes. This is not like me, she told herself. I'm just like this today because I haven't quite figured out how to get back to my normal self.

Finally, she picked up her phone and called the florist she always used; sending people flowers was her standard way of wishing people happy birthday or thanking them for hospitality.

'White and blue, please, Nina,' she said after

giving her Orson's name and the ward and room numbers. 'Not a tall thing, just a little friendly-looking bouquet. And on the card please put, "Sorry, had to go away unexpectedly, see you soon. So pleased you're getting better. S." And then another one to the same ward. This one is to be addressed to the nursing staff and I want the card to say "I've had to go away unexpectedly on urgent family business, but if I don't see you again, my sincere thanks for your kindness to Orson and myself. Saskia." Make that one bright but not too big – I don't know how much room there is in their office. Do you still have boxes of chocolates to add to orders? Oh, good – send the biggest box you have to the nurses as well.'

She put the phone down and sat vacantly staring at the empty water glass, and tried to imagine what might happen when she next met Orson. Not that she saw him in the building very often, perhaps every three weeks or so, but it was bound to happen. Would he recognise her with her new hairstyle? And why did she only see him so rarely? It hadn't occurred to her before that it was unusual to only see your immediate neighbour every few weeks. She crossed paths with the people in the flat to her right at least once a week, either in the lift or in the parking area under the building, or at the entrance. After a few minutes of looking back she had a pattern emerging in her mind. She only ever saw Orson if she was heading out for dinner or getting into or out of her car in the evening, and once they had shared the lift. He only goes out in the evenings, she thought, perhaps he works from home and then he goes out to meet friends at night. I'll stay out of his way for now.

Chapter 18

After a frustrating half hour of putting things on and then pulling them off and throwing them on the floor the morning after Henry cut her hair, Saskia decided she must get some new clothes, or at least tops and maybe a dress or two. She had never before considered whether hairstyle had anything to do with clothing style, but now she discovered that those two things were closely linked. Clothes she had happily put on when her hair was long and thick, now looked wrong. It was hard to decide why those tops and dresses looked out of place, but they did, and she realised that to do justice to the new hairstyle she must go shopping.

Saskia often set out to go shopping with a friend, sometimes for a particular item she needed and at other times just for the sake of maybe buying something that took her fancy. Her friends invariably complained loudly when she suddenly declared that she was bored, that she couldn't stand going into another shop and suggested going for a cup of coffee instead.

'What is it with you?' exclaimed Marian one Saturday morning. 'You keep doing this! I call you and we chat and then *you* say, let's go shopping – and then when we've barely started, you say you're tired of shopping. I just don't get it!'

'I'm sorry!' said Saskia repentantly on the last occasion she went out with Marian. 'I always start out full of good intensions, because I want to get something new to wear, and then I just get overwhelmed by all the displays and the millions of choices, and going in and out of different shops, so I just give up.'

And Marian had laughed and given her arm a pat. 'Ah well, I got to see you, even if the shopping didn't work out. One day I'll make you keep going until you actually buy something. But never mind, let's go and have coffee instead. And at least it got you out of that lonely flat.'

And Saskia had once again wondered why people felt she ought to feel lonely, because she worked from home and lived alone. As if they didn't believe her when she said her stories and characters lived in her head, or maybe she lived in their made-up world, and she never felt lonely at all. Maybe that's why I'm writing a novel about an author, she thought, so people will understand how it works.

It was Tuesday, which meant it might be one of Lizzie's half days off, so Saskia decided to call her and ask for shopping advice, because despite Lizzie never going out with men, and never wearing anything smart or putting on make-up she had real fashion sense. Saskia could remember untold occasions when Lizzie passed a critical comment on somebody they saw in a cafe or when they went for walks. 'Totally wrong,' she would say after glancing at a woman they met. 'She should never have put on such a long top with those wide pants, she's too short and it makes her look very short-legged and box shaped.'

The fact the Lizzie was short-legged and box-shaped herself was neither here nor there, her own lack of style was unimportant. The crucial thing was that she had impeccable taste and a great sense of style when it came to others.

'I need help,' said Saskia when Lizzie picked up her call. 'I've just *got* to buy some clothes, and I need you to help and advise me please.'

'Really? And you're not going to do that silly thing, when you suddenly say you're bored with shopping and how about we have coffee instead?'

'No, no, I promise I won't. This time I must get a whole lot of things at the same time. Nothing in my wardrobe, apart from pants and jeans, feels right anymore. I've got nothing to wear on my top half apart from some t-shirts and merino jumpers. Is it your half day off? Can we go out this afternoon? I'll take you to lunch first. I'll meet you outside the library and we can have lunch somewhere downtown. Or perhaps at the City Art gallery across the street – I like the food in the café there. Let's meet outside the Art Gallery!'

At quarter past twelve, Saskia disbelievingly watched Lizzie risking her life by crossing wide and busy Wellesley Street straight across from the library to the art gallery instead of using the pedestrian crossing, somehow avoiding getting bowled over by the multi-lane vehicles racing for the traffic lights. But the admonition forming in her mind never got voiced, because Lizzie walked right past her and disappeared into the foyer. After a moment of standing there baffled, Saskia grinned and followed, catching up as her friend was slowly scanning the space, trying to see if Saskia had arrived before her. Coming up from behind she said, 'Hi, Lizzie! I was waiting outside.'

Lizzie turned around and stared. 'Oh my God, you look so different – gorgeous, the hair! I hardly recognise you.'

'You *didn't* recognise me! You walked right past me without a second look. And the hair is why I need new clothes, or some anyway. This style makes a lot of what I have look wrong, but I can't tell what it is I need, so you'll have to help me.'

After lunch, Lizzie took charge and said, 'Right!

This time there's going to be no faffing around being indecisive and giving up before we've even started. We're going to all the shops I *know* have the right kind of trendy gear, and you're just going to do what I say, right?'

'OK,' said Saskia meekly and held back a smile at the tone of Lizzie's voice, like that of a strict nanny, or what she imagined a strict nanny would sound like. 'But how do *you* know which shops to go to? You never buy anything trendy yourself, if you don't mind my saying.'

Lizzie smiled with sly amusement. 'But I window shop – a lot! I love the kind of clothes I don't have the figure for, so I often walk into shops and check things out, look at the latest styles. I know exactly where we'll go. And also, which you probably don't know either, some of my other friends take me with them for advice when they go clothes shopping, and a lot of the shop assistants know me.'

What followed after lunch was exactly what Saskia had hoped for. In each shop Lizzie told her to go into a fitting room and take her clothes off, and then a stream of outfits would be delivered to be tried and commented on, often involving a shop assistant, who if she didn't already know, would quickly realise she was dealing with a styling expert. And then the assistant would exchange short and sometimes mysterious opinions with Lizzie before going off to fetch something else.

'Hellooo!' said Saskia loudly at one stage in the third shop. 'I'm still here! Remember me?' Two faces swung briefly towards her, then they went straight back to critiquing the dress she had just put on.

Having moved from one end of town to the other by taxi and ending up in Parnell, Saskia put her pile of carrier bags on the ground, hugged Lizzie and said, 'You're amazing! Thank you! I could never have achieved this without you. You're my personal stylist now and I'll never buy anything if you're not with me.'

She got out of a cab at her apartment at half past five with nine bags from six different shops, completely exhausted.

That night Saskia did the biggest sorting out of her wardrobe she had ever done. Why had she brough everything with her when she moved from her house? she wondered. Why hadn't she sorted and discarded then instead of just taking all her clothes, some of which she hadn't worn for fifteen years. By the time she had emptied her wardrobe and every drawer, the bed was no longer big enough to spread things out on. She contemplated the piles on the floor and tried to decide where to start. After a few minutes she went to the get some rubbish bags and discovered she was nearly out of bin liners. 'Stuff it!' she said aloud and tried to think of what she could put things into to take to the charity shop, or to throw out. But nothing came to mind, apart from the bags her new clothes had come in and there wasn't enough of them. The job, which she had thought might take an hour before dinner, kept her busy to half past ten with a short break for cheese on toast instead of dinner.

When it was finally done, her wardrobe had spare hanging space, something it had never had since she moved in, her clothes were grouped by what kind and season they were, her drawers were tidy and not overfull, and the hallway was lined with piles of neatly folded clothes. After making a note on the pad beside the fridge to buy rubbish sacks and wondering where the nearest charity shop was, Alba sat down with a glass of wine and some crackers and started reading Leanne Moriarty's new book on her Kindle to celebrate.

After reading the message from Marian on Saturday night Saskia changed her plans for Sunday without a thought for the approaching deadline for submitting the first draft of the new book. It was nearly finished, after all, another few thousand words and she would have tied up the loose ends, and dispatched the character, who was scheduled to die, to a watery grave. After that she'd do some editing and that was it for now. She had got so much done during those days in the hospital, all that quiet time between reading a passage out to Orson now and then, talking to him and going for short walks in the corridor. Amazing what you can achieve when there are no distractions, when you say 'no, thanks' to lunch invitations and coffee dates for two weeks, and there is nothing else to do. A picnic lunch at Silo Park with Marian and Anna was irresistible, particularly after turning down the Sunday lunch invitation the previous weekend.

At half past ten on the Sunday morning Saskia was waiting outside her block of flats equipped with her wide-brimmed straw hat, a canvas bag with a birthday present for her goddaughter, Anna, who was turning six in a week, and a bottle of sunscreen in her bag.

'We're going away on Anna's birthday this year,' Marian had said a couple of weeks ago. 'She wants to go on a boat, so we're taking her to Waiheke on the ferry and staying the night in a B&B where the little cabins are down a steep path on a slope among nikau palms, it looks amazing. I'll be in touch about meeting up before then – it will be the first birthday since she was born that you haven't spent the day with us.'

Marian and Anna arrived with two little friends of Anna's, and they set out with the three little girls running ahead like small flock of shrill birds, talking and laughing, a formation that stayed the same until they had crossed the bridge over the yacht basin.

Suddenly Marian stopped mid-sentence of telling

Saskia about her mother's hip operation and yelled, 'Hey, girls, stop! Take your shoes off!'

She turned to Saskia. 'I forgot about those damn steps - they went down there the last time we came here. The green slime is irresistible.'

They sat on the top step watching the girls take their sandals off, go down the wide tidal steps until they were in water up to their knees and then shuffle about with delighted squeals, running their feet through the slime on the lower steps that were constantly under water.

Silo Park was busy as usual on a sunny Sunday. Marian spread the picnic rug she had carried over her arm in the shade under a tree and took her little backpack off. 'They'll be busy now,' she said and started getting plastic containers out. 'We'll just leave the lids on until they suddenly discover they're starving.'

When Saskia took her straw hat off Marian did a doubletake of surprise. 'My God, you look like a stranger! I haven't seen you with short hair since we were at intermediate school. Fabulous look, it really suits you - and blond streaks! Wait till Anna spots you without the hat, I'll bet you ten dollars I know exactly what will happen. She'll say, "but now I won't be able to braid your hair!" as if you had long hair just for her to practice on.'

'I never thought of that,' said Saskia untruthfully.

'What a shame! And it will take ages to grow out again.'

But of course, she had thought of that, remembering the many times at home or in a café or in the car when Anna's little fingers had been busy tugging and getting tangled in her hair. First she learnt to make a braid, then she got increasingly good at it and made many thin braids, and recently she managed a complicated braid with the help of a video clip on Marian's phone. In Saskia's bag was a heavy box wrapped in birthday paper and inside the box was a hollow head made of glass and a wig of long hair for Anna to braid. And she can wear it for dress-up games or fancy-dress parties too, thought Saskia now, but why didn't I leave it at home and just run up and get it when we get back there, how silly!

True to predictions, Anna and her friends came to get something to eat, and Anna stared at Saskia. 'You look pretty!' she said. 'You look different, like a girl – a grown-up girl.'

But when all the food was eaten, and all the play equipment used and re-used the girls were hot and tired, and Marian decided to take a taxi back to Ponsonby. 'They're too tired to walk back to your place in this heat and take the bus again,' she said. 'Look at them, they're drooping, we'd never make it. Are you happy to walk back or would you like to come in the taxi, and we'll swing past your place.'

'No thanks, I'm fine - I'll enjoy the walk, I might

even stop for a paddle in the slime on the tidal steps. Now, I'm sorry to load you down, but in a taxi it won't matter so much. This is Anna's present but take the canvas bag, so it's easy to carry. You can give it back some other time.'

She had been acutely aware the whole time she had been with Marian that nothing had been said about Tony, but presumably that meant all was well. Maybe Marian didn't want to revisit her earlier suspicions and felt embarrassed about having called Saskia in a panic and told her.

As soon as she got home she had a long cool shower, put her kimono on and sat down to kill off the character, who had originally been destined for a watery grave, but walking along the wharf had inspired her and now she thought she might let him crash to the ground from a giant crane. Never pass up an opportunity to add blood and gore for a bit for dramatic effect, she thought and smiled at the thought that she might never need to think of a way for someone to die again, once this book was finished.

That evening Marian texted: *I forgot to tell you the rest of the drama/saga. All well and very funny conclusion. Tell you next time we meet, funnier in person. Mx*

Chapter 19

When Matthew called on the Thursday morning to change the time for their lunch date, he was very apologetic. 'I don't like to treat my favourite author like this,' he said, 'but I've got a surprise for you, and it involves waiting for a phone call at twelve or a bit after. So rather than maybe keep you waiting, I thought we could have a late lunch at quarter or half past one - if it's OK with you.'

'Fine,' she said and smiled at the phrase "favourite author". 'I've got nothing else to do all this week than write books and have lunch with you. And don't fib about my books, I know you don't really like crime novels. Your previous partner told me just before he retired, but he said I should move over to you anyway because you're so good. Which has turned out to be right.'

'No, that's not quite accurate.' Matthew sounded

defensive. 'I usually don't like crime novels, not most of them. But your characters are so different, even the evil ones, that I find myself completely engaged in what they do, so I do like your books.'

'That's nice, thank you! I'll be there at quarter past one, and I've got a surprise for you too.'

She put the phone on the kitchen bench and went to stand in her favourite thinking spot by the balcony door, where she could see the paved area with trees below the building, and the quayside on the far side with the boats tied up. In daylight the view was so different from at night. The harbour bridge was just another structure now, it didn't dominate the view the way the arc of lights did at night and being able to see right across the water to the North Shore suburbs was like looking at a picture with houses gleaming white amongst the green.

She wondered what Orson could see from his balcony around the corner, but she couldn't quite picture it, so she might have a look on Google Earth. His apartment must be vast, first from beside hers to the corner, then down half the other side of the building. And just then, as if conjured up by her thoughts, she heard a noise from his flat. The building was built to be extra soundproof, which was a thing that had attracted her in the first place, but she occasionally heard noises from what she presumed was Orson's kitchen.

He was back! She stood there for a moment frozen

in place, once again in that dislocated state of mind that she had experienced in the hospital, like an ability to see two images side by side. On the one hand, the reality of the man she didn't know, who lived just through that wall, and on the other hand, the man she had looked after and cared for, the unconscious man in a hospital bed. She suddenly felt like crying, swallowed hard and went to look in her wardrobe, to decide what to wear out for lunch. Not that she particularly wanted to impress Matthew, but her new hairstyle had made her very aware of what she wore, how clothes either fitted or didn't fit the new look.

Saskia could see Matthew hurrying along the wide paved walk along the quayside and nearly waved to direct him to where she was sitting a under a gigantic striped sun umbrella at the Wynyard Pavilion. Then she decided it would be more fun to see if he would recognise her, so she took her sunglasses off, picked up her Kindle and continued reading, as if she hadn't seen him. Out of the corner of her eye she watched him scanning the tables first one way and then the other, then he disappeared inside. A couple of moments later he was back in the doorway, his gaze skimmed right over her, despite the fact that she was now looking in his direction, and she began to feel sorry for him. Getting to her feet she called out, 'Matthew, over here!' and he literally jumped with surprise. How gratifying, she thought, I've never made anyone jump before, and stayed standing as he approached. He looked her up and down with disbelief written on his face and said, loudly enough for the couple at the net table to look over and listen, 'My God, Saskia! How amazing – what did you do?'

She discarded a naughty impulse to say, "what do you mean, what did I do?" as unkind, the game was over. She sat down after being kissed, put the Kindle to one side and smiled. 'Nothing invasive or expensive, Matt. No scalpels or injections of any kind. I had a haircut and some blond highlights, that's all. I found a fabulous guy who really knows how to bring out the best in a woman, and then our friend Lizzie, the style guru, took me shopping for new clothes.'

'I'm staggered – it's such a transformation.' He laughed. 'I'm not meaning to be insulting, but to go from quietly pretty woman with non-descript hair to someone who looks absolutely stunning and ten years younger, amazing! Can't wait for you to have some new author photos taken.'

'I'm not sure about that, now you mention it.' Saskia frowned and looked out over the water while she thought of it. 'No, I don't think so, not yet. I'll just enjoy feeling like somebody else for a while first. Tell me your surprise. Are you going to go and live in England, in Oxford?'

'What? Oxford? Where did you get that idea?' He

looked puzzled along with that slightly worried look he sometimes had when she was playing with him.

'I just thought you might go and live there some time,' she said casually. 'Wear a corduroy jacket with leather elbow patches and smoke a pipe and sit around discussing existentialism or something. Or not?'

'If you are going to tease me right through lunch I might not tell you anything at all,' said Matthew, but he was smiling as he said it. 'Now listen to this - I've got you a Netflix deal, or very nearly! An eight-part series, they think, but you must finish the book you're writing before they sign a proper deal and pay the real money. They love the first two books, and they know you're writing book number three and the money's very good, correction, will be very good, they've only taken an option so far.'

'Oh great!' said Saskia with possibilities she was not going to voice instantly popping into her mind like firecrackers, and new plans forming in the back of her head. 'That's really excellent, thank you Matthew! I promise never to tease you again if this goes through.'

To her surprise he reached across and put his hand on hers. 'If you're going to promise anything, please promise to continue teasing me. I know I frown, but you're such fun and nobody else teases me apart from my husband - I don't know why.'

This was a side to Matthew she had never suspected, and she studied his face for a few moments trying to work it out, then she grinned. 'OK, of course I'll tease you. To tell you the truth, it's nearly impossible to resist. Or it was, because I always thought you got a bit embarrassed, which was so funny and sweet. Do you want to know why nobody else teases you?'

Now he looked worried again, or maybe the expression she had taken for worry was more one of secret amusement, some kind of self-protective cover to hide how much he enjoyed being teased. 'And why is that?'

'Two things, I think. You never tease other people, do you? That's probably one reason why others don't tease you. Most people are probably more restrained than I am in that respect. *And* it might be because you look so serious and intellectual that they think you wouldn't like silly jokes.'

'So that crack about Oxford was because of how I look? My God, Saskia, this is such an eye-opener. I had no idea I look like that. I mean, I don't dress like some 1930's Oxford highbrow.'

'It's probably just me.' Saskia patted his arm and decided to change the subject. 'Probably nobody else sees you like that. I think it's lovely, please don't ever change. Now, let me tell you my surprise!'

'Have you done something mad again?' Matthew's look was half amused, half suspicious. 'Any more strangers rescued or maybe suing you?' He noticed her look and laughed. 'Yes, I can see how guilty you look, which totally confirms what I've suspected all along. Some man you *vaguely* know? How does that work? No, don't try to explain it because it doesn't work. And the way you talked about him so affectionately. You didn't know him at all, did you? So, how the hell did it happen?'

Saskia felt her composure crumble, her eyes filled with tears and Matthew's expression changed from teasing to concerned. 'Oh, God, Saskia! Are you crying? I'm sorry!'

She wiped her eyes and tried to smile. 'I can't talk about it, I really can't. I think my heart is broken - and yes, I know it's cliché, but my heart really feels as if it's got a big crack right through it, and if I tell you the whole story I'll cry for real. I'll tell you my surprise later.'

What she wanted to do was change the subject, but all at once she knew she couldn't continue, she must leave. 'Sorry, I have to leave, this is not the day to tell you – I'll talk to you later.'

Despite his guilty protests and how agonised he looked, she got up and walked away, putting on her sunglasses to hide her eyes from people who might have overheard her voice crack when she spoke that final sentence. She pulled the sunhat down over her forehead and manged not to cry until she was inside her flat. After half an hour she texted Matthew: *Sorry, I accused you of not teasing people and then you did, and I ruined it. Not your fault! S x*

.   .   .

It took only a few days for Saskia to change her mind about having a new author photo taken. The reaction to her new look had made her re-think her ideas, and after some out-loud discussion with herself in the shower one morning, she decided to do it. But as this new photo would probably not only appear on the back cover of the third book in the series she was just finishing, but also on the books in the new genre, she wanted to own it. If she had to change publisher for these new books, she wanted the photo to go with her, to be used in advertising and PR for the women's genre books and possibly be recognised as the same person who used to write crime-novels. I've got a following, she said to herself, so let's use it to get some initial traction, at least some readers will be curious to see what I can do in another genre than the one they're used to.

Not that she couldn't have yet another photo taken for the new books, but she usually got nervous and self-conscious when she was about to have a formal photo taken and nearly invariably felt the result made her look uptight and unnatural. She remembered with vivid embarrassment the last time her publishers told her they wanted the photo updated. The poor photographer showed her one after another on her little camera screen only to have them rejected, until finally shot number twenty-four made Saskia feel she looked like a normal human being. But looking at herself in the bathroom mirror, she realised how much more confident she felt with the new hairstyle and the amazing things it did for her face; maybe a new photo would more easily achieved.

On a hot and muggy morning, with levels of humidity more like the tropics than New Zealand, Saskia set out for the Countdown Metro supermarket in Halsey Street. She was just about to go in when she thought how nice it would be to pop in to see Henry, so she picked up two take-out coffees and two almond pastries at the café instead and continued along the street. He might be busy, she thought, but she could sit in the background and read a magazine until he was free, and if his coffee got cold he would still have a nice pastry.

Carefully balancing the two mugs and with the bag of pastries gently clamped under her arm, she pushed the door open and found herself looking at Orson lying back in a proper reclining barber's chair getting a shave. Henry lifted his hand with the razor to see who had come in, and quick as lightning Saskia shook her head, then put the mugs on the magazine table and held her forefinger across her lips and mouthed a silent "no". To his great credit Henry just nodded calmly and went back to the business of shaving, and Saskia sat down, picked up a random magazine and spent the next ten minutes looking unseeingly at an article about body building.

She more felt than saw Henry glance over at her a couple of times, and she could imagine what would be going through his mind, that she was planning to give Orson a surprise, jump up and hug him or something cousinly and affectionate. But just Henry raised the chair back to vertical, she caught his eye and again mouthed a silent "no" and shook her head. She could see how puzzled he was now, as she remained seated, still looking down at the magazine until Orson had paid and left without a second glance at her. Getting to her feet she said quickly, 'Thanks, Henry! I need to explain, so if you have nobody else due in the next few minutes, can we please sit down with our cooling coffees, so I can confess.'

They sat in a comfortable hairdresser's chair each, swung towards each other and after a while Henry got up from where he had sat listening, mesmerised and only interrupting with the occasional question. He looked down at her face with an odd expression.

'I can't believe it!' he said. 'Are you crazy? Why did you do it? You say you didn't want him to be alone, but what the hell does that mean? There would be medical personnel all around him and then his friends would turn up. I just don't get it — two weeks sitting in his hospital room, organising for him to be shaved, talking and singing to him and you don't even know him!'

She could see how confused he was about her now. They hadn't known each other long, but she felt they had connected as friends, not just via a business transaction, and it was important to make him understand, even if she didn't fully understand her decision herself.

'I don't know,' she said slowly, choosing her words carefully. 'I know I said I didn't want him to be alone, but it wasn't a decision based on some fact. It was just a very strong feeling, nearly overwhelming. I mean, I didn't know him, and I still don't. I'd only met him very briefly in the building, we had never had a conversation.'

She paused and looked down at her hands. 'This is going to make me sound insane, I know, but when I was kneeling there in the puddle of blood, holding on tight to his head and pressing that wadded up towel against the wound, I talked to him, even though he wasn't conscious. I just knew he was very lonely. Somehow the certainty crept up my arms from where my hands were clasped to his head – this guy is utterly lonely, he's got nobody. And I was certain that I didn't just imagine it. The feeling was nearly like spoken words in my head, as if I were being told about his loneliness.'

She finished talking and looked up at Henry, still towering over her with a strange look on his face and he put his tattooed hand on the top of her head. 'Saskia, my friend - you're psychic, you must be! That explains it. You felt his loneliness when you touched him.'

'Don't be silly, Henry! Of course, I'm not psychic. I'd never had an instinct like that in my entire life before then. It's just a mystery, or maybe I'm just a bit mad.'

'Call it what you will, it's just another word for the same thing. I have no doubt at all,' said Henry with total conviction. 'I'll make some fresh coffee, hot this time, to go with our pastries that we haven't even touched. I've got eight minutes before the next appointment, but she's always late.'

On the way back to the supermarket on the corner, Saskia thought of what Henry had said and laughed to herself, amused but also slightly worried. Maybe she was psychic, but only when she touched people's heads? Or only when someone was injured and really needed her help and she touched them? Or, and this was the worst idea of all, only with Orson. God help me if that's the case, she thought, because then I'm doomed. I'll have to live next to him possibly forever, and occasionally we'll meet on the car park level or in the lift, but we'll have no further contact. How dreadful it would be if I believed I am psychic only in relation to him, to know that and never kind of expand on it.

It wasn't until she was walking home with her shopping that the follow-on thought occurred to her, that perhaps the most hurtful thing of all was that he would never know her. He obviously knew that someone, who called herself his cousin, had been with him all that time in the hospital, and he might have found out that it was the same person who found him, but she couldn't even begin to imagine what he would make of it.

From Henry: *Orson sent txt asking who you are, says he vaguely recognised you. What do I say?*

From Saskia: *Tell him my first name, say you don't know my surname pls.*

Chapter 20

The call from Wendy at the hospital took Saskia by surprise and for a moment she couldn't think who Wendy was.

'Hi Saskia, it's Wendy. Sorry to call so early,' she said, 'but I think you should know about this. I got your number from Orson's notes – you're down as his next of kin, of course. We've had a woman here who seemed a bit odd. Well, very odd to tell you the truth. She was asking about you.'

'How strange,' said Saskia cautiously. 'What did she want to know?'

'She came in yesterday during visiting hours and asked to speak to someone who had nursed Orson, so I talked to her, and I got suspicious right away. She wouldn't tell me her name, she said it wasn't *her* name that was the issue, she wanted to know who *you* were. So, I said, a nameless visitor and you expect me to know which one you mean? Just to test the waters a bit, you know, find out if she was a bit crazy. And she said she'd been told some woman spent a couple weeks in Orson's room, all day every day, and she wanted the name of that person.'

'And what did you say?' asked Saskia, wondering if some irate relative was wanting to sue her for pretending to be a cousin of Orson's and for filling in that consent form on his behalf. 'Did you tell her my name?' And then she thought this might seem a strange thing to say, so she added, 'Not that I mind, but I can't imagine who she would be and if she seemed a bit crazy ...'

'God no! Of course, I didn't tell her your name, or that you were down as his next of kin or anything at all. I didn't like the way she was demanding information, and I reckoned that if she had any right to know who had visited Orson she should ask him, not us. I said we can't give out details like those, Orson's visitors are his business, it's private. I tried to find out how she knew, but she wouldn't say – might be one of the cleaners or an orderly, anyone who comes and goes in the ward. Or she overheard a nurse talking in the café, could be anything.'

'So, you have no idea who this person might be?'

Wendy laughed. 'Plenty of theories in the nurses' office, but we don't know. The favourite theory is that she's a discarded woman friend or partner, and she's stalking him - and that's my favourite guess too. Who else would do this kind of thing?'

'What did she look like?'

'Mid-forties, dark, slim figure. *Very* expensive looking clothes, fabulous shoes. Do you want to see a photo of her?'

'You have a photo? Really? How on earth did you manage that?'

'One of the other nurses overheard the conversation I had with her in the little visitors' lounge, you know, that bay off the corridor at the end of the ward. She said she didn't like the tone of the questions she heard when she passed, so she walked past again with her phone in her hand and snapped a shot – not perfect, but good enough. I didn't even realise what she was doing, I saw her phone raised and heard her say something, so I thought she was talking to someone on speaker as she waked down the corridor, but she was just being clever. I'll get her to message it to you now. She's on this morning.'

Saskia put her phone down and tried to imagine how this had played out. If someone had told the unknown woman directly about Saskia being in Orson's room day after day, then surely the woman would have asked that person about her identity, so it couldn't be one of the nurses, they all knew her name. She could have overheard someone talking about it, as Wendy had said, but what were the odds of a chance comment about someone you know being made in your hearing by someone you couldn't ask for the details? Too much coincidence, thought Saskia. It would never stand up as a plot in a book. Too lose, it must be something else, some more definite link we don't know about. Someone knew I was there, and that person also knew this woman had some connection to Orson and told her. But only that I was there, not who I was. Irritated by this vague but intriguing story, she got out of bed and went to have a shower.

The photo was on her phone within an hour and the moment she looked at it she knew she had seen the woman before. The picture showed her three-quarters full on, her head just slightly turned to the right and something about the way she held her head seemed very familiar. Dark hair in a shoulder length bob, a high-necked blouse under a tailored jacket and a pencil skirt. Saskia and decided to save the image to her laptop and do some research.

On and off during the rest of the day Saskia looked at the woman's face in the photo. She sharpened as much as she could and tried to manipulate it to get the clearest image possible. She was definitely familiar, but not someone she had ever talked to, so maybe someone she had passed in a shop or on the street. She closed her eyes and pictured the face in her mind, but nothing came to her until she went to bed that night when she suddenly knew where she had seen the stranger. Outside the apartment building, and more than once. Wendy was probably right, the woman was a stalker, but what was her connection to Orson?

I'll do a search on the internet tomorrow, thought Saskia and scrunched up her pillow to achieve the best lying-down reading position. I'll get to the bottom of this one way or another. She picked up her Kindle and reached over to turn her bedside light off the way she did every night when she read herself to sleep, and the Kindle would shut itself down after ten minutes of her not turning to a new page.

Chapter 21

After only five minutes of searching for information about Orson's stalker the next day Saskia found her name. She used Orson's name to search and the first couple of dozen hits were about an old jazz musician who was also called Orson Dankworth, but then she struck gold. Orson's name appeared in an article about the global financial crash, when he had been one of several asked to comment, then again a few years later when he was the speaker at a conference in Sydney, where he was described as an 'international authority on the pitfalls of hedge-funds'. A bit further down she found a link to a Facebook page, which she clicked on and there was the answer. On the page of the woman she recognised as the stalker, was a link posted by her to another article about Orson, this time about crypto currencies. The stalker's name was Cindy Porter, she lived in Auckland and had listed herself as a company director, which in Saskia's head equated to 'occupation unknown'. She looked at the posts on Cindy's page but learnt nothing about her relationship, if any, with Orson. Maybe she never had a relationship with him, she thought, maybe she just wanted to, but it never happened, and she became obsessive, or perhaps someone she knew dated him or had been married to him. It was impossible to guess and there seemed to be no way forward, so Saskia turned her laptop off and went for a walk in the warm rain that had plagued the city for the last two days.

A couple of days later when Saskia returned from the supermarket with the kefir she always had a glass of at lunchtime and had run out of, a voice spoke just behind her when she was about to run her card over the sensor pad beside the front door.

'Excuse me,' said a woman's voice. 'Do you live here?'

Saskia knew before she turned around that this was the woman from the hospital, Orson's stalker. There was a demanding tone to the question, as if she felt that she was entitled to an answer and not prepared to be brushed off.

'Yes, I do,' she said calmly and slid the key card back into her jeans pocket. 'Can I help you?'

'I wonder if you could let me in. I'm visiting Mr Dankworth and he didn't hear the signal when I used the entry phone, he's not picked up.'

'Who is Mr Dankworth?' asked Saskia, choosing the safest and easiest option to de-escalate a potentially difficult situation. 'I don't recognise the name.'

'He's lived here for a couple of years,' said Cindy Porter and moved closed to the door as if to step in beside Saskia as soon as she opened the door.

'If he's not responding to the entry phone he's probably out. Why don't you come back later?'

And then an idea flashed into her head, and she said, 'Hang on, what does he look like? Is he that very dark guy, back hair, tall and a bit stocky – early forties?'

'Yes!' said Cindy Porter and now she smiled. 'That's him! I'm coming for lunch, but as I said, I can't get in.'

'But he doesn't live here now!' said Saskia. 'Didn't he tell you? He must have sold the apartment because he moved out a few days ago, last Friday I think it was, or it might have been Saturday. Yes, it was Saturday – I had to wait ages at the entrance to the parking level because the damn removal truck was blocking the way.' She shook her head as if still annoyed at the memory. 'God knows why they took his stuff down in the lift to that level, but that's what they did.'

She glanced at the list of residents and said, 'Oh God, they've done it again, they've not removed his name yet. I must remind them.'

'Oh no! Are you sure?'

'Oh yes,' said Saskia, still calm and trying to sound as if this conversation was beginning to bore her. 'I probably spent fifteen minutes sitting there watching them load his damn armchairs and stuff. Listen, I must go in, my kefir is getting warm in the sun. But it was definitely he who was moving. He came down in the lift and talked to the removal guys as I sat there waiting. I didn't know his name, of course, but there's only one man who fits that description who lives here – or who lived here, I should say.'

'He sold the apartment?' Cindy Porter sounded disconsolate. 'Do you know where he was moving to?'

Saskia raised her voice, as if out of patience and no longer bothering to be polite. 'Of *course*, I don't know where he's moved to! I just I *told* you, I don't know the man, I only knew him by sight, didn't even know his name. And may I ask why he didn't tell *you* he had moved if he invited you for lunch? Or why you don't call him? Surely if you know him, you must have his phone number! This whole thing seems very fishy to me! I don't think you even know him.'

Cindy Porter turned on her heel and walked away without another word, and Saskia looked after her until she disappeared around the corner before she let herself in. Wendy was right, the woman was stalking him, and now she must warn Orson without revealing her own identity. As soon as she was inside her own apartment she texted him, blessing the fact that she had got his phone number at the hospital when he was admitted. He would have no idea who sent the text, it would just arrive from a number with no name attached.

'Mr Dankworth, a woman called Cindy, who I think is stalking you, tried to get into the building. I told her you had moved. If I'm wrong please call her and apologise from me.' She didn't sign the message and pressed Send.

The reply came half an hour later: *'Thank you. I saw her on the CCTV and didn't respond. Who are you?'*

After some thought she replied: *'Just a concerned tenant. Not keen on people trying to get in on flimsy excuses.'*

There, she thought, and poured herself a glass of vanilla kefir, that's taken care of that. Let's hope she never turns up here again.

Meeting with Lizzie and Marian together was one of Saskia's favourite things, but it didn't happen often enough. She felt that fate had been unkind when arranging these two perfect friends for her. They lived miles apart, neither of them anywhere near Saskia, and they worked such different hours that coordinating them was difficult. Lizzie had perfectly ordinary business hours at the library in the CBD, apart from working some weekends, and Marian alternated between being on the early shift and the evening shift at a private hospital, and in her time off she had a child and a husband to spend time with.

But today the three of them had managed to coordinate themselves to meet on a Tuesday afternoon at the Wintergarden café on the Domain when Lizzie was free, and Marian had two days off. Saskia arrived after a brisk forty-five-minute walk to find that her friends had both arrived before her and were standing outside the entrance immersed in an animated discussion about Wayne Brown, sometime controversial mayor of Auckland.

'Oh, please!' exclaimed Saskia when she realised what they were talking about. 'Can we agree not to talk about him and ruin lunch – please?'

Lizzie stared at her, and Marian started laughing. 'Are you still in that nearly demented state about him?' she asked. 'Get over it - he's just another old, up-himself white guy who thinks he knows everything, soon to vanish over the history horizon. A pontification maestro.'

'But such fun to talk about,' interjected Lizzie. 'He has perfected that untouchable business leader approach, you know, he doesn't act like a man in a position where he's accountable to his voters or the general public, he acts like the CEO of some global corporation. Such hubris! And a terrible communicator, too – remember those floods?'

Marian turned to Lizzie and said in a low voice behind her hand, 'You might not know this, but Saskia has a medical condition, a severe allergy reaction to Brown's name, or anything being said about him. She comes out in a rash and becomes incoherent. We'll talk about him another time.'

They sat outside with a shared platter full of delicious things, and Saskia was amused to see how fast the other two had formed the kind of friendship that most people only develop after years of knowing each other's taste, habits and family. Lizzie and she had done the same thing a couple of years earlier when Matthew introduced them, so maybe it was she who was the catalyst that made this happen so easily, and she did appear to have a lot of close friends.

This thought led Saskia on to thinking about how relatively few close friends she herself had, very few, and how she had formed that crazy connection with a man she didn't know, an unconscious one at that. But maybe, she continued her meandering thoughts, while the others kept talking, maybe it's also because I spend so much time on my own and I'm happy with writing and total silence. Suddenly she realised that Lizzie and Marian were both silent and looking intently at her.

'What?' she said. 'Did you say something?'

'God, she's done it again!' said Marian and started

to laugh. 'Yes, Saskia, we did say something, or more correctly, several things. While you were looking at the tree over there and daydreaming. Were you writing a book in your head?'

'I want to tell you something,' said Saskia, having made a snap decision that now was a good time. 'A kind of confession, so you can tell me what you think. I'm going to stop writing crime novels.'

'Is this anything to do with those cover image photos you were talking about ages ago when you were looking at photos online? Does Matthew know this?' asked Marian.

Saskia shook her head. 'No, he doesn't, not yet and you're not to tell him, absolutely not. I did start telling him just recently and then … something happened, and I had to leave very suddenly, and I never told him, but I will.'

She saw Marian's eyes on her and continued quickly before she had time to start digging into why she had never got around to telling Matthew. 'I'm writing a novel in the so-called women's contemporary fiction genre, but that probably isn't the official term, it's just how I think of it.'

'What's it about?' Lizzie was instantly interested, because she didn't read crime novels and had once said she had only read all of Saskia's because she'd feel disloyal if she hadn't read them. Saskia recalled the conversation about compensation porn she and Lizzie had a few months earlier, when they discussed modern romance novels, but she knew Lizzie wouldn't refer to it. Discretion was her middle name.

'It's basically about life, love and the universe,' said Saskia. 'About women and their relationships with those around them – parents, siblings, lovers, friends. How things impact on their lives, how things go wrong, or right. How life can change in a heartbeat, and how finding out something from the past can alter your world view.'

'Is there lots of sex?' asked Marion. 'Or will they be straight novels. And what's the one you're writing about?'

'They have minimal sex, mostly implied - they kind of stop at the bedroom door, or not very far into the bedroom, anyway. I found writing about sex tedious. When I started writing the first one, during the Covid lockdown, I read twenty or more of those modern romance novels on my Kindle to see what they were like, and I found them so over the top descriptive with detailed sex scenes every thirty pages or whatever. And I mean minute detail, like anatomical dissection. Enough to put you to sleep in five minutes. I like sex, but to me it's something I like doing, not something I want to write about.'

'So, what's it about? Who is the woman and what does she do, and what happens to her?' Lizzie was in full question mode now, and Saskia said, 'Well, the one I'm writing right now, which is actually the third one in this new genre, is about a woman crime writer, who changes genres and starts writing women's fiction instead, and the book *she* writes is about a woman crime writer who changes genres and starts writing women's fiction instead.'

There was a short moment of silence while Marian and Lizzie glanced at each other and then they were all laughing, out of control, with two couples at a table nearby staring at them.

'The literary equivalent of those Russian stacking dolls that fit into each other,' cried Lizzie with tears of laughter running down her cheeks. 'Hilarious!'

Yes, exactly, thought Saskia, Matryoshka dolls. I had some when I was little. She remembered taking them apart and finding yet another and then another, ever smaller until the last one, only as big as the tip of her finger, and then she lost the tiniest one and was inconsolable.

When they had calmed down again, Marian asked hesitantly, 'Are *we* in it?'

'Don't be an idiot - of course, you're not in it! It's not a real story, it's just a way for me to have some fun instead of having to pay minute attention to the plot and timeline and who knew what when, and all that stuff you have to be so careful with when you write crime.'

Saskia felt a smile break out even just talking about it. 'These books are like full-on creative freedom. I can make my characters be anything I like. The first one I wrote is about a woman who's totally reckless, she's got no sense of self-preservation at all. She takes risks and acts on her impulses, but she's also smart and educated and knows how things work. Some will say she's a contradiction, but she's not - she's just a bit random and funny and a risk-taker.'

'She sounds exactly like you! But tell us some more about this latest one,' said Lizzie. 'You're obviously having fun writing it, so intricate with that stacking doll theme, if I can call it that. What's the most fun part?'

Saskia drank some of her now cold coffee and tried to think of how to describe it. 'It gives me a chance to have some gentle fun with some of the things I read in interviews with other authors. For example, I make this woman say to a new acquaintance that she's probably not a real writer, because she doesn't write during set hours and she doesn't have a fancy desk with a gorgeous painting on the wall in a special writing room, she's just a pretend writer. And it's got a bit of satire about editors and publishers' contracts. But in general, the best thing is how *happy* it makes me to write these stories, it's such fun!'

'Matthew's in for a surprise, then.' Lizzie looked thoughtful. 'I wonder if he's going to approve.'

'I don't care,' said Saskia. 'I don't give a shit, as they say. I can change agents, or just market them as ebooks on Amazon, and I can self-publish them. My contract with the publisher is up for review in a few months, so I might just leave if they don't like it.' She waved her slice of ciabatta in the air to emphasise her point. 'This is my reward for having worked hard, met deadlines, had little or no say in cover design and had my suggested back cover blurbs dismissed for years and years. I'm changing my whole writing life and it feels marvellous.'

Towards the end of a couple of hours, just when they were looking at their phones to see when they might be able to schedule another date, Saskia dared ask after Tony. Doing it now, with Lizzie present would enable Marian to just reply casually with a 'He's fine' or something like it and no further information would be expected.

'Say hi to Tony from me,' she said. 'I haven't seen him for a while, we've all been so busy.'

'Hey, I forgot to tell you!' exclaimed Marian and turned to Lizzie. 'This will amuse you too, such a crazy story. A while ago I thought Tony was having an affair because he had these mysterious so-called meetings on Wednesday nights. I told Saskia I thought he was having it off with his pretty secretary, and she provided a nice little test, which seemed to put that worry to rest. But on our wedding anniversary last week, he said we'd go on a mystery tour, he'd organised the babysitter and I had to wear a nice dress and high heels, preferably a dress with a full skirt.'

She was smiling as she spoke and Saskia felt

hugely relieved, because this was clearly not going to be a story about unfaithfulness.

'So, I did what I was told,' continued Marian, trying not to laugh. 'He took me to a place called the Just Dancing something, to a ballroom dance evening for their students. He'd been taking dancing lessons!'

Now Saskia was laughing too. 'For God's sake - Tony dancing, I can't imagine it! How did it go? He never seemed remotely like a dancing guy to me.'

'I know, but despite me loving to dance and having spent two years learning all those different dances when I was a teenager, including the tango, which is huge fun, I did marry him. And now, after nine years, we can dance together. And it was such a glamourous event, they had lovely lighting and great music and all these people dressed in suits and gorgeous dresses, and I met some new people.'

Saskia walked home again rather than accept a ride. She felt she needed time to reflect. It had clouded over now, and the cool air on her face was calming, a sensation she needed. For some reason Marian's story had made her feel sad, as if she had missed out on something, some vital component she had never previously missed. Maybe it's a little midlife crisis, she thought, as she walked down Parnell Road to get to the waterfront, a more pleasant way home instead of through the CBD. Maybe I'm at the age when suddenly things take on a new importance, things like not having children, no long-term partner or any of those things that Marian has, wedding anniversaries and whatever. But halfway home her spirits rose, and she discarded the thoughts that had so surprisingly popped up and smiled at the prospect of going home and continuing writing.

Chapter 22

When the lights went out Saskia was on the car park level after putting a bag of rubbish into the dumpster outside instead of dropping it down the rubbish chute. Having initially set out to pick up something from her car, she had absentmindedly taken the bag with her to the garage level. She had just got back in, and the self-closing man-gate had shut behind her when everything went dark, inside and out. She realised that she had never been in total darkness since she was young, when the Auckland had been struck by a power outage on a scale that affected everything. All she saw through the gates were the headlights of a couple cars before they disappeared around the corner and then there was no light at all.

She moved slowly sideways until her outstretched hand touched the front of a car and followed the line of cars to the right where the stairs were. As her eyes acclimatised she saw low-level light through the little window in the emergency stair door and heaved a sigh of relief. At least she wouldn't have to struggle up three floors in a pitch-dark stairwell. If only she had taken her phone, but it hadn't occurred to her that she would need it. When she got to her level she would be able to feel her way to her front door and then inside until she could locate her phone and light some candles. To make herself feel less tense she started singing *Did you ever see the rain?* and the acoustics of the stairwell suited her voice, which boosted her morale.

Just as she put her foot on the bottom step of the second to last flight of stairs, the lights went out there too, and she was left in darkness as thick as a black blanket. She stopped singing and felt that creeping fear she hadn't experienced since she was a child, that there was something or someone right behind her. The chill of the unknown swept cold fingers down the back of her neck. She told herself to stop being silly, and started singing again, the way she often did when she was on her own and closed her eyes, which made her feel better, a different kind of darkness than looking into a dark void with open eyes.

With her hand on the stair rail, she climbed slowly to her landing, ran her hand along the wall and pulled open the door to the lift foyer, still singing, and a man's voice said, 'What's that song?' Her eyes flew open. Orson was standing just a few steps away, holding his lit-up phone.

'It's called *Did you ever see the rain on a sunny day?*' she said after a moment, and he said, 'You're Saskia.'

'Yes.' She didn't know what to say after that. His voice had not expressed anything in particular, and she hoped he wasn't going to tell her how outrageous it was that she had hijacked his life when he was unconscious, taken liberties with his rights and breached his privacy. In her mind she could nearly hear what he would say, the tone of disapproval and maybe anger. But all he said was, 'Just stay here, please.'

She stood as if frozen until a few moments later he reappeared with a lit lantern held high. 'I was about to go in to get this and come down to rescue you when I heard you singing on the stairs.'

This was having like a conversation with the Cheshire cat, thought Saskia. 'How did you know I was down there?'

He smiled, the first smile she had ever seen on his face, and it made her want to smile too, as they stood there with the light of a camping lantern casting strange shadows over their features, surrounded by inky black darkness.

'I wasn't spying on you,' he said, 'but I'd just come in with some shopping. I always go in the evening when the supermarket is quiet, and I dumped the bags in the kitchen and went back to close the door and saw the lift door closing behind you. I thought the bag in your hand would be rubbish and I noticed you'd left your door ajar.'

'Aha!' she said and laughed quietly, suddenly relaxed. 'And then the lights went out.'

'I went back in and unpacked some of the shopping and then, as you said, the lights went out. I took my phone to light the way and went to check if you'd come back up, but your door wasn't closed, so I thought if you weren't stuck in the lift, you might have got locked out downstairs – so I was going down to rescue you.'

This might be the perfect opportunity to defuse the whole hospital story, she thought. He didn't seem angry or upset and maybe she could make her behaviour seem reasonable. Not that she could immediately think of how to achieve this, because the way she had planned to do it before he left the hospital suddenly seemed silly, but it was worth a try.

'Would you like to come in for a glass of wine or something? And bring your lantern, please, because I don't have one.'

'Let me put my frozen dinners in the freezer first,' he said and handed her the lantern. 'Take this - I've got my phone to light the way.'

He disappeared into his flat leaving the door open, and Saskia went into hers leaving her door open too, wondering with a sense of slight apprehension where this was going to lead. She had a lot of explaining and apologising to do, and how she handled the next few minutes might prove vital if a permanent problem was to be avoided. The thought of messing up this opportunity and forever be cringing at the thought of meeting him again made her feel stressed. She lit the four tea candles that always sat in their little glass bowls on the windowsill in the living room and put two of them on the coffee table. She still had no idea what she was going to say to him, her mind was a blank.

After a moment's thought she left the lantern on the kitchen bench and put a bottle of red wine and two glasses on the coffee table, but then she didn't know what to do with herself. Sitting down and waiting for him seemed strange, like being a person on a stage set, pouring the wine before he got there was not an option until she knew if he drank red wine or any wine at all. When he came in she was still standing in the middle of the room looking towards the door, still indecisive and it was too late to try to look casual.

He walked right up to her and took her shoulders in a strong grip. 'Thank you!' he said and pulled her against him for a moment. 'You might have saved my life or at least my sanity.' He held her away, looked closely at her and smiled. 'You've changed your hair - very pretty! I saw you at Henry's, but I didn't realise who you were, and I didn't know you live here.'

They sat opposite each other with the little coffee table between them, studying each other across the candle flames and neither seemed to know what to say. After a few moments of silence Saskia asked if he drank red wine, and he said coolly, 'Of course, I drink red wine. It's every pirate's favourite drink.'

She blushed when she remembered that Henry had quoted her to Orson, handed him a glass and started speaking very rapidly in order to get it out of the way.

'I owe you an apology – or several. I took some terrible liberties and kind of infiltrated your life. I lied to the ambulance staff and to everyone at the hospital and to Henry - *and* I signed a consent form about allowing them to perform surgery on you, if necessary, and give you blood. I said I was your next of kin, though I had no right to do that. I'm very sorry, it was a completely mad thing to do. Did they tell you my name?'

She had spoken very fast, keen to get to say what she needed to say without interruptions, but he seemed quite relaxed. 'Yes, I know what you did, brilliant idea. I've been thinking of trying to get in touch with you to thank you, but I've hesitated. I didn't know how you got to be there, and I wondered if there was something my head injury had made me forget. I thought I might just embarrass both of us. I didn't know we're neighbours until just now. I've never noticed your name anywhere.'

'It's on my mailbox downstairs,' said Saskia. 'That's how I knew what to tell the hospital and the ambulance crew. Our mailboxes are side by side, so I knew your full name.'

He shook his head and was quiet for a moment, as if he was hesitating, then he said, 'I asked Henry about you. I'd found out a few things from the nurses before I was discharged, when you suddenly didn't come back, so now I know quite a lot about you. I know the card that came with the flowers said you had to go away, but the nurses were disappointed that you didn't come back at all before I was discharged. They left your little table in my room, hoping you'd return. And I can't thank you enough for doing what you did. But why did you give up so much time on a stranger?'

She couldn't think of anything that would make sense. At best her reasons would sound odd and at worst mad, and the silence stretched out between them like a taut rubber band, which she felt might snap at any moment, but she still couldn't think of anything to say.

'Saskia,' he said gently. 'Look at me. What's the trouble? *Is* there something I should know, something my head injury has made me forget? What happened the day I fell? What did I do?'

Oh, God, she thought, now he thinks it's *his* fault that I'm so tongue tied, I must say something. 'You didn't do *anything*! It's all my doing because I thought you'd be lonely. That's why I did … what I did.' She hesitated for a moment and added quickly, trying to make it sound rational, 'I felt as if you were my responsibility because I was up late that night, and I heard the lift door beeping, so I went out and found you and did what I could. And then I couldn't just let them take you away. I mean, you might have woken up and felt so dislocated and confused, and it … worried me. So, I went with you in the ambulance.'

'The staff at the hospital said you sat there writing all day every day alternating with talking to me, making phone calls, and eating lunch - and you sang to me, they commented on your lovely voice. And I remember that. As soon as I heard you singing on the stairs just now, I knew it was you. You sang that song at the hospital, didn't you - and another one. You sang both very slowly and softly.'

'I was worried I'd wake you up if you were asleep inside your head - if that's possible – so I kind of turned a couple of songs into lullabies. Songs that lend themselves to being sung like that, very slowly and softly.'

'There was another one I recognised, and I can still hear it in my head.'

'It could have been *Time to say goodbye*, I sang it to you sometimes when I was leaving at night. Or maybe *I will always love you* – it's a Dolly Parton song. They used it in The Bodyguard with Whitney Houston belting it out like it was an anthem, but it's a really sweet song, quite sad. I sang it to you because it's such calm, lilting melody when it's sung slowly. I thought it was soothing and kind of like a sign for you that you weren't alone.'

Not until that very moment had it occurred to her that she had repeatedly sung a love song to him, and she quailed at what he might think. But Orson seemed unfazed and lifted his glass in a toast. 'I would never have recognised you with your new hairstyle – I remember you with longer hair from when I first woke up and you told me to say we're cousins. And I know you sang that Dolly Parton song many times, it kind of triggered something in my head when you did. I knew someone who cared was there in that strange white space in my head.'

They sat in silence for a while and Saskia thought how restful this was, that she felt no need to say anything apart from answering his questions, and how odd it was that he didn't seem to resent her intrusion into his life.

Suddenly he said, as if he had just remembered, 'You read to me! Was it from one of your books? The nurses told me who you are, of course and I couldn't understand why you had stayed there with me, and I had no idea we were neighbours. I can't remember the words of what you read, just that you were obviously reading out loud, not just talking. I can hear the rhythm of it now.'

'It was from the book I'm writing at the moment. I sometimes read things I write aloud to myself, particularly dialogue. I can always tell when it doesn't sound quite right, even if it looks ok on the computer screen. But mostly I read things to you to provide a bit of change. I'd move my chair closer and have the laptop on my knee and read a few paragraphs – just to give you some stimulation.'

'Amazing – thank you!'

'Did you hear everything all the time?' She felt herself blush as she tried to remember what she might have said in the phone calls with Matthew and a couple of her friends; those calls when she never let on she was sitting in someone's hospital room, apart from that one time with Matthew on the last day. Chatty conversations about this and that but possibly forgetting at times that he might not just be able to hear her voice, but to understand.

'Oh, no – I'm sure I just regained some awareness now and then when my mind kind of surfaced, but it seemed to be linked to your voice. Which is something I've only realised in retrospect. I've hardly any impression of the voices of nurses or doctors at all.'

Ah yes, she thought, that's very cleverly put, but I still don't know how much he remembers from those phone calls, or maybe things I said to him. Perhaps he doesn't want to embarrass me, which is very kind, but I hope I didn't say anything totally inappropriate.

When he was leaving he stopped in the doorway. 'When I was getting dressed to go home, there was a clean white shirt on a hanger in the wardrobe, and I asked them if the hospital had washed the blood out and they said you must have don't it – you were the only person who'd been in my room.'

'I did and I'm sorry, Orson, I really am. I meddled in everything and invaded your privacy. That first day I was trying to see if I could find someone to notify, because they'd told me there was no next of kin on your records, so I was looking for your wallet and phone, looking for clues. Without telling the nurses, of course, because they thought I was your cousin. I kept your phone charged with my charger in case anyone sent a message, you know how you can see them even on a locked screen on your phone? How did you know the shirt had been bloody?'

'Unfortunately, my phone is set to not show notifications, but the backlog's been dealt with now. The nurses told me about the state of my shirt. How on earth did you get the blood out? I didn't think it was possible.'

'My grandmother taught me some tricks when I was teenager, when I went through a period of having nose bleeds and ruined one white school shirt after the other. My dad didn't have a clue.'

He surprised her by pulling her into a hug, held her tight against his chest with both arms around her and spoke very quietly against her temple, she felt his warm breath through her hair. 'I would have been so lonely inside my head without you there.'

And Saskia felt that strange sensation again,

similar to what she had experienced when he lay bleeding on the floor, when she held his head with both hands.

'I knew you were lonely,' she said very quietly. 'I could feel it. That's why I did it.'

Chapter 23

It was a few days now since the night the power went off, when Saskia and Orson drank red wine by candlelight and got to know each other in a more conventional way, as she thought of it. And she did think about it quite often, sometimes to point of distraction. Her thoughts covered many aspects, some of which she might never get answers to, but she desperately needed to reach some clarity about the phenomenon she thought of as the loneliness current.

What was that strange feeling, the current that crept up her arms as she knelt on the floor by the lift, the sensation Henry had said was proof she was psychic? And if she was, then she must find out what it meant. She had gone through her reasoning again and again, trying to reach a conclusion. Had she felt Orson's loneliness so strongly when she held his head in her hands because he was injured? Or was it because she was touching his head? Or was it because it was Orson and would never have happened with anyone else?

She tried to think if she had ever touched anyone else's head, and yes, of course she had, many times in the changing room after netball when she used to undo her friend Marian's ponytail because her frizzy hair always got stuck in the tie and had to pulled out slowly and carefully. She used to hold Marian's head steady with one hand and gently pull strands of hair free with the other. But there had never been any strange sensations going on then, and neither did she feel anything other than affection when she touched her goddaughter's head. The one remaining explanation, the one she hoped was the right one, was that it was due to him being injured, the only injured person she had ever attended to and not something linked directly to him as a person.

And I *was* right, she thought, he was lonely and would have been utterly lonely in that hospital room without me there, because not a single person came to see him or enquired after him. So, it was good that I somehow knew right from the moment when I first touched his head that I must stay with him.

Another confusing thing was the wine date with Orson in the black-out, and the way he had hugged her. The way she hadn't felt it was strange or unexpected but relished it. As if they had hugged many times in some distant past they were not consciously aware of, in some other place or time, familiar and safe. Often when someone hugged her, particularly men, she felt slightly awkward, overly conscious of not getting into too much full-body contact, not too much of the "hands flat of her back" and brining her breasts into contact with someone's chest. But that had not happened with Orson, which was strange. When he hugged her tight that evening, she felt safe and comfortable, and it was only afterwards she realised that her whole body had been pressed against his.

Perhaps the thing she felt most conflicted about was how she had replied to his whisper in the middle of that tight hug, 'I knew you were lonely - I could feel it. That's why I did it.' Why on earth had she said something so revealing and open to interpretation, so personal, and she cringed at what he might think of her now. Maybe he would avoid her, think she was slightly unbalanced and overemotional.

The worry circled in and out of her mind and reappeared at intervals throughout the day and even in her dreams. What did these confusing elements mean? Those strange and unsettling little words, the intense feelings and the incidents involving Orson combined to make her wonder about herself and, as a consequence, about Orson, too. Was there something that linked them, beyond the practical and visible things that happened in his hospital room? I have to stop this, Saskia told herself repeatedly but without much effect. Thinking about it was driving her mad, and when she looked at it the way an outsider would, from a realistic angle, she was appalled at herself. She didn't even know the man, she just imagined she did, and she must be careful, remind herself that he was basically a stranger, so she didn't reveal her inner conflict next time she saw him, because she might embarrass him and leave herself open to being talked about as a someone as crazy as the stalker.

When Orson knocked on her door one morning a couple of days later, he apologised for possibly disturbing her during her writing time which made Saskia choke back a laugh. She always found it amusing to tell people the truth when they assumed she wrote during certain hours each day or had some sort of schedule regarding days and times.

'Oh, I'm not a *real* writer,' she said to Orson, who was probably wondering why she nearly laughed. 'I don't think I can be because I write in bits and pieces when I feel like it or think of something, no set routine at all. I take a break and do the ironing and get side tracked into tidying my wardrobe, leaving the hero dangling by his fingernails from a cliff edge for an hour. I can write anywhere, even in a hospital room. I'm probably just a pretend author.'

'Definitely not,' he said. 'I know a lot more about you now. I've done some research and you're definitely not a pretend author. But that aside, would you like to come to my place for a coffee, if it's not interrupting anything, or maybe this afternoon?'

'I'd love to,' said Saskia. 'Now?'

'Yes, now is good.'

She picked up her keys from the hall table and followed him to his flat, which she had so often speculated about and wondered how it was laid out and how far he could see from his second balcony around the corner of the building.

But all thoughts of balconies and views were pushed to one side and forgotten when she saw his living room, which was huge, at least twice the size of hers or even more. There were probably just as many pieces of furniture as in most living-cum-dining rooms, but still a lot of empty space. While Orson made coffee and put two Danish pastries on a plate, she kept glancing around the large room. It's like he's divided it up into two spaces, she thought after a moment or two of consideration, it's just that he's done it much more deliberately than most people would. There's a huge gap between the sofa and armchair group and the dining table and sideboard side. I like it – very uncluttered and it doesn't feel as if it's half-empty, it feels spacious and kind of calm. He's a bit different in more ways than one.

They sat on his balcony on the same side of the building as Saskia's and she wondered what he could hear from hers, despite the balconies being recessed into the walls. Her mind flew back to the day she stood leaning on the balcony rail talking to and looking down at Bruno. What if Orson had been sitting on his balcony at the same time, or if he had the balcony door open?

As if he could sense her thoughts, he said. 'You know that day when the handsome guy came back and stood under your balcony and called you?'

'Yes?' She could feel her face grow hot. 'Did you hear the conversation, my side of it, I mean?'

'I heard both sides,' said Orson and looked as if he was about to start laughing but holding it back. 'His voice carried quite well. I liked the way you handled that, a very classy performance. He had to stand there listening to you listing all his misdeeds with a crowd stopping behind him to listen too, and he couldn't leave, or you wouldn't have told him the PIN to unlock his phone. I realised after a moment that he'd borrowed one to call you. Such an entitled guy.'

Saskia suddenly clicked. 'Was it you who refused to let him in?'

'The big ape? Yeah, that was me − only a few minutes before he called you. I came across him outside when I was coming back from a walk. He tried to tell me that he was expected by a friend, and he'd forgotten the door code, but I didn't believe him. Why didn't he just use the door phone to call up? I told him to fuck off, because I thought he was probably the guy you sent packing before – very effectively done, that time too.'

'Oh, God!' exclaimed Saskia and now she knew her face was beetroot red. 'You heard me screaming like a banshee, I'm sorry!'

'Why? You've got nothing to be sorry about, nothing at all. You were staunch and strong, a great performance both times. And I particularly enjoyed watching the woman who filmed him while he pleaded at ground level, and you listed his crimes quite loudly from three floors up. Well, several people were filming the scene from behind and to the side of him, but this particular girl went right around him, holding her phone up the whole time, so she would get his face. I bet she caught the lot, the entire conversation. Every now and then she swivelled up and filmed you too.'

Saskia started to laugh and had to put down the mug she had held frozen halfway to her mouth, so it wouldn't spill.

'Are you kidding? I didn't even notice anyone listening, much less filming the whole thing, I was full of white-hot anger. And now it's probably on social media somewhere.'

He looked silently at her with a little smile, expecting something, and she said, 'What? Did I miss something?'

'If it's on social media, which I think we can take for

granted, then sooner or later it might reach someone who knows you, and they'll love it and forward it to everyone you know, and it's bound to go viral, if that's not happened already. But no harm done, they'll think you're amazing, just like I did. It might end up on newspaper websites and on YouTube, who knows? So be prepared, learn to enjoy it. But the key thing you didn't think of is what it will do to him if his other women get to see it. Then all three will know about all three, so to speak. Imagine how much trouble he'll be in.'

When they finished laughing he said, abruptly and out of context. 'You touched my face.'

She didn't know what to say, just sat there in a silence that got more intense by the second. Not just an absence of sound, but a silence so full of thoughts and unspoken emotions that she felt it like a physical presence. The fact that he remembered it made her feel as if she had touched him inappropriately, and maybe she had, though at the time it was to comfort him, not for her own gratification.

And once again he said, as he had over wine in her flat, 'Saskia, look at me. It was great, don't be embarrassed. I felt your fingers on my face more than once and even though I wasn't thinking, not the way I do when I'm conscious, I kind of knew I'd be all right. That someone was there and looking out for me.' He hesitated for a second. 'And I felt it was somebody I knew well. I know it sounds mad, but I did, and I still do.'

She changed the subject away from personal things by asking how long he had lived there and was grateful that he didn't bring up his time in hospital again. When she was leaving he pulled her into one of those hugs that made her feel she was in the place she was always meant to be, in a familiar and comfortable place. They stood there for a minute or two and then she pulled back slightly, and he loosened his arms. 'Too much?'

'Oh no, I could stand here all day. I just wanted to look at you.'

He chuckled. 'No, we can't stand here all day, worse luck. I have to finish a report I've only half written, but I had to see you first.' He kissed her forehead and let her go.

As she walked through the door, he said casually behind her, 'Did you love him?' She turned, looked straight into his eyes and replied with great certainty, 'Oh no, not at all, but I was taken in by the charm and the face – lust, I think.' She left him laughing.

Chapter 24

After days of hesitation about when and how to tell Matthew about the new books after her abrupt and emotional exit from the café, Saskia found that the opportunity was given to her without any effort on her part. On Saturday morning Matthew called from downstairs and asked if he could come up for a coffee. Saskia, who was standing in the kitchen making a shopping list and eating toast at the same time, dressed in trackpants and a T-shirt, had no time to agonise or prepare. She pressed the street door button, left her plate and the shopping list on the bench, and went to open her door.

Matthew had only once before been in her flat and had never approached her in a weekend, so she waited for the lift to arrive at her floor with a slight feeling of apprehension. When the lift door slid open

Matthew stepped out with a bouquet of pink roses in one hand and a little brown paper bag in the other.

'I've come to apologise,' he said, as he followed her inside and handed her the flowers. 'I've been feeling so guilty, I couldn't just call you, I had to come over.'

Saskia was nearly overcome with guilt at his heartfelt statement. She put the flowers on the table, and reached out to give him a hug, another first.

'Oh, please don't, Matthew, it wasn't your fault! It was just me being over-sensitive and emotional and acting like an idiot. Please don't feel like that! Let's sit down and have coffee and we'll talk about it. Did you come alone or is what's-his-name, your husband, downstairs waiting for you?'

'Joe - he's sitting on a bench looking at the boats, he's perfectly happy,' said Matthew. 'Don't worry about him.'

Saskia ignored him and went to the balcony and looked down. There was only one person sitting on the bench outside the entrance, so she put her hands around her mouth to make the sound carry and yelled, 'Hey, Joe! Yohoo! Look up!'

The man on the bench turned, got to his feet and advanced, looking up at her and she nearly laughed at how ridiculous this was. 'Come on up and have a coffee!' she called down to him. 'I'll open the bottom door for you – level three.'

'OK!' he called back and headed towards the

door, and Saskia walked past Matthew, who was standing where she had left him in the middle of the room, pressed the door button and turned to find him laughing.

'Really, Saskia!' he said. 'You're the most impulsive person I've ever known.'

They sat in the living room with the glass sliding door to the balcony open and had coffee and the little cakes Matthew had brought, and after the usual exchanges when you meet a new person for the first time, there was a pause. Matthew was just opening his mouth to say something when Saskia got up and said, 'Just a moment, this won't take a second.'

She picked her phone up from the kitchen bench and dialled Orson's number. 'Hi, sorry this is a bit unexpected, but do you want come for a coffee, right now – this very minute?'

She turned back to Matthew and Joe, who were sitting side by side on the sofa looking slightly confused. 'Someone I want you to meet,' she said breezily and went to open the door before returning to the living room.

This will defuse the whole thing, she thought, while she watched the two men watching her. Orson will come straight in here and probably give me a hug and the whole thing will be like a scene in a book, entertaining and funny.

When she heard Orson's footsteps in the hall she went to meet him, right up close and it worked just as she had hoped it would. His arms reacted as if on their own accord and he enfolded her in one of those hugs that she loved. She kissed his cheek, laughed and broke free.

'Hi, Orson!' she said. 'I want you to meet Matthew and Joe.'

'I heard you inviting strange men up for coffee by shouting from the balcony,' said Orson and shook hands with Matthew and Joe. 'She's getting famous around here for her balcony conversations with men who're on the ground. Pleased to meet you.'

'Matthew is my agent, and Joe's his husband,' said Saskia from the kitchen bench where she was making a coffee for Orson. 'I wanted you to come and meet them because Matthew and I ended up with a bit of an emotional scene in a café not long ago – we were talking about you.'

She turned with the coffee mug in her hand, took in the expression on Matthew's face and said, 'Matthew, let's untangle all this now, for you and Joe – and partially for Orson as well, and then we'll all feel better.'

Over the next hour, with frequent interruptions, a lot of questions and surprised intakes of breath from Matthew and Joe, the story unfolded. Saskia started from the moment she heard the lift beeping that dramatic evening, how she found Orson in a puddle of blood and how she was convinced she could feel his loneliness, continued to the lies she told at the hospital, then on to the phone conversation she had with Matthew while she sat holding Orson's hand in his hospital room. She then went on to describe the scene in the blackout, when she opened the stair door singing and saw Orson standing there, and how he knew she must be Saskia. And finally, they reached the end, after Orson has filled them in on how he had heard her singing and talking to him while he was in a coma, and how he knew who she must be when he heard her singing on the emergency stairs.

Matthew looked from Saskia to Orson and then back again, his face awestruck. 'That's the best story I've heard in my entire life - better than any of your books, Saskia.' He turned to Orson. 'I hope you realise how unique this woman is – I think they broke the mould when they made her.'

'You should write it up as a book, or part of a book because it really is amazing,' said Joe, sounding quite serious. 'Drama and devotion, if you don't mind me calling it that, and then such a discovery – in total darkness. And the singing. I can see the film playing out in my head as we speak.'

Instantly Saskia realised that this was the moment, the perfect opportunity to finally tell Matthew, so she smiled at Joe and said, 'You don't know how right you are, Joe! I'm right in the middle of writing the third book in a new genre, that even Matthew knows nothing about yet. I was about to tell him the day I had the melt-down in the café, but I ran away before I had got to it.'

She felt Orson's glance and said, 'I'll tell you that part later, Orson. But to get back to the new genre, I want to tell you right now Matthew, because this is the perfect moment. And I want to say at the start, that if you don't want to represent these books, then we'll just be friends, because it's a huge departure from crime writing, and you might not want to have anything to do with it.'

She hoped she could present this well. Not that she was trying to sell the idea to Matthew, she just wanted to inform him, but she also wanted to explain why she was so happy about the change.

'These books are what I think of as women's contemporary fiction,' she said and directed herself straight at Matthew, as if the other two weren't in the room. 'I think of them as stories about life, love and the universe - not necessarily in that order. About women and the people around them, family and friends, lovers and hangers-on. About how your life can change in a heartbeat, when things to go right and or when something goes wrong.' She turned and smiled at Orson who she could feel was watching her intently. 'And they're about links to the past, and how finding out something from the past, good, bad or downright criminal, can alter your view of family, or parents and even change your entire world view.'

She could see that Matthew was about to

comment and said quickly. 'And here's another thing for you, Joe. The book I'm writing right now, the third one in this genre, is about a crime writer, who changes genres and starts writing women's fiction instead, and the book *she* writes is about a woman crime writer who changes genres and starts writing women's fiction.'

Laughter erupted from two directions and left Matthew sitting silent and looking pensive, and feeling sorry for him she reached out from her chair to pat his arm. 'Too shocked to speak? Do you want to read them?'

'I can't wait!' he said energetically. 'Particularly the one about the writer – what a crazy idea, it's nearly about yourself, isn't it?'

Perhaps he hadn't been stunned or dismayed, thought Saskia, perhaps he was already thinking ahead about how to pitch these books, he's such a clever guy.

'No, it's not about me at all,' she said, 'it was just an amusing idea I had for a story. And I'm leaving Orson out of it, he's suffered enough violations of his privacy from me, though he's been very nice about it, actually – much nicer than I deserve.'

'She has nothing to apologise for, she saved my sanity and possibly my life,' said Orson calmly. 'But I think I'd rather not be written into a book.'

When Matthew and Joe had left and Saskia was putting the roses in a vase after making Orson another cup of coffee, she said, 'This new genre, the books I've written so far, they make me so happy.'

He studied her face for a moment before he said, 'Weren't you happy writing before?'

'Oh, heavens yes! I'm nearly always happy when I'm writing, but this is different. I did tell my two closest friends, Marian and Lizzie about this recently, and I tried to describe it to them, the difference. It's like I've been hemmed in by the rules and disciplines of crime fiction for years and years. The way things have to hang together, logic and how things evolve etc – crime readers love finding holes in the plot or pointing out some anomaly. But this is total creative freedom, like walking through an unexpected door into a garden I didn't even know was there.'

After another hug Orson went back to his place just before lunch to continue the article he had been writing when she called him, and Saskia sat down with a sigh of relief at having finally told Matthew. She would send him the first two books and then wait to hear what he thought, but his verdict felt unimportant now. Just telling another couple of people about these books had confirmed in her mind that this was what she wanted to do. She could make people laugh or cry, and she didn't really mind if people called these books lightweight or some other slightly denigrating phrase, this was what she wanted to do.

Chapter 25

Saskia leaned into the backseat of her car and a sudden, sharp pain in her ankle made her utter a sharp little scream before she bit her lip. What on earth had she done?

'What's wrong? Did you hurt yourself?' Orson's voice came from the far end of the row, and she steadied herself against the door, turned her head and saw him standing behind his car with a large flat packet in his hands.

'I just twisted my ankle,' she called back. 'I'm fine.' But when she put her foot on the ground that sharp twinge of pain hit her again and she yelped. With her weight on one foot, she leaned against the side of the car and waited for the pain to stop, feeling ridiculous and helpless.

'What did you do?' Now he was right beside her and there was no sign of the parcel.

'I was just turning to get stuff off the back seat,' she said crossly, 'and somehow I twisted my ankle, very sudden and painful. And it hurts when I put my foot on the ground. Will you be my walking stick, please?'

'Where are your keys?' She pointed at the keys she had dropped on the back seat when she had leaned in to get her bag and the pain hit her. He reached in, picked up her bag and the keys and locked the car. 'Here, hold this.'

He handed her the shoulder bag and the keys, got a remote out of his pocket and clicked it; she heard his car locking, way down there at the end of the row. Before she understood what he was going to do, he bent, put one arm behind her knees and the other behind her back and lifted her.

'Let me go! Put me down!' she said, outraged and embarrassed, as he carried her towards the lift. 'I'm not a baby.'

He chuckled, and she could tell he wouldn't listen, he was enjoying this. 'My turn to take a few liberties, I think. Now press the button.'

She pressed the lift button, he settled her more comfortably against his chest and when the lift appeared he got in and said again, 'Press the button.'

Saskia pressed the button for level three and said nothing. Her dangling foot caused pain to jump in her ankle at every move, as if a knife was being repeatedly poked into it. At her door, he turned so her left hand was close to the door and said, 'Unlock it, please.'

When he finally put her down in the middle of her living room, holding her steady and watching her face, she cried out and felt tears pool in her eyes as soon as she put the foot on the floor. He picked her up again, deposited her sideways on the sofa and carefully arranged her feet to rest side by side. Suddenly she was sobbing. 'God, it hurts!'

She wiped her face on her sleeve and tried to pull herself together. Being helpless and injured was not something she found easy to adjust to after a lifetime of perfect health and never a single injury worse than bruises.

Orson disappeared and she wiped her eyes again and thought she wasn't surprised. A crying woman would probably send most men running, but then he was back, and she realised he'd just gone to close her front door.

'Let me look at it.' He didn't wait for an answer, just crouched beside the sofa and took her shoes off. Lifting the injured ankle, he held it steady with one hand and moved it gently from side to side. Saskia bit her lip and smothered a groan as he rotated the foot, still slowly and gently. There was a little click and suddenly the pain was gone, and contrary to logic and reason, she burst into tears.

He continued to hold her foot in a warm grip and

fished in his pocket for a handkerchief. 'Here,' he said, 'use this instead of your sleeve. I'm sorry I hurt you.'

She sniffled and smiled at the same time. 'You didn't hurt me, you fixed it - the pain's gone! It just vanished when it clicked like that, and I don't know why I'm crying. Did you hear it - the click when you turned my foot sideways? How did you know how to do that?'

'I didn't. I wish I could claim I did, but sadly not, it was just dumb luck.' He smiled and put her foot back on the sofa, got to his feet and said, 'Stay there and I'll get some ice.'

'I don't have ice,' said Saskia. 'I don't like ice in drinks, so I only make some when I have visitors coming.' She thought for a moment. 'But there's a bag of frozen broad beans on the second shelf in the freezer.'

A few minutes later she had a bag of frozen beans wrapped in a kitchen towel draped over her ankle, a glass of water in her hand and Orson was sitting companionably on the floor beside the sofa. Impulsively she reached out and put her hand on his cheek. 'Thank you!'

He captured her hand against his face and held it there. 'I've been wondering if I'd ever feel that touch again.' He moved her hand, kissed her palm and put it back on her thigh. 'I've got to go down and get some stuff from my car, so please stay here until I get back, will you? Just in case you walk on it and fall over when you're alone here. Is it OK if I take your keys so I can get back in?'

'Of course - and thank you! Now we're even, we've both rescued the other.'

'I don't think so.' He got up. 'It will take a bit more than this to even the score. I'll be back soon.'

When the door closed behind him she looked at her hand, now with the fingers folded over the palm as if to hold on to his kiss and wondered if this could be love. It wasn't lust because Orson wasn't sexy to look at, he was chunky and swarthy and a bit like a pirate, or maybe a bear, but there was something about him that made her want to keep close to him, to lean into that steady body and be held. The way she picked up on his feelings, the same way that she had felt his loneliness through her hands, that was something she had never experienced with anyone before. The feeling of his heartbeat when he hugged her had made her want to put her arms around his neck and kiss him, hold him tight and make him happy.

When Orson returned and found Saskia standing by the kitchen bench putting things on a tray, he shook his head. 'I should have known! You weren't going to sit there and wait, were you? What are you doing?'

'I just wanted to try my foot to see if it's working properly. And it's perfectly OK again. So, seeing it's after five now, I thought we could have a glass of wine.'

'Let me take that tray,' said Orson after watching her add a bottle, two glasses and a bowl of olives to what was already on the tray. 'I'd hate for my promised drink and those nice things to end up on the floor. Do you want to sit on the balcony?'

'Oh yes, let's,' she said and then instantly changed her mind. 'No, no, wait – maybe we shouldn't. Let's sit inside it's probably better in case ...'

'In case of what?' said Orson looking hard at her. 'What's this about?'

Before she had time to think of a reply, she saw the exact moment he realised. He put the tray on the coffee table and said, 'It was you who sent me that text message about the stalker, wasn't it?'

'It was before you knew I was the crazy woman next door.' She poured a glass of wine and handed it to him. 'I thought I'd better stay anonymous in case you came to thank and me or to explain why you had a stalker, or something. And then you might recognise me and tell me off for lying to the staff at the hospital and for all those intrusive things I did.'

'Which I'd never do, you know that. But how did you know she might be a stalker? Was it just the way she behaved?'

Saskia took a sip of her wine, thought it over and decided it would be best to tell him the whole story. 'A nurse from your ward, Wendy, called me and said that after you were discharged a woman had been there trying to find out who I was. She'd heard from someone that I was sitting in your room every day, but not my name and she was pressuring Wendy to tell her. So, Wendy thought she should warn me, because the nurses thought this woman was a bit unbalanced. And that was good, of course, because she turned up outside one day when I was about to swipe my card and tried to get me to let her in.'

'History repeats itself,' said Orson and grinned. 'And you told her I'd moved? Great idea! She's been very persistent for a while now, and I've blocked her on my phone. Did she believe you?'

'I'm an author, Orson! I can create a scene from nothing without thinking. I said I didn't know anyone by your name, and then I pretended to realise who she might mean, so I described you, and said you had moved a few days ago. And she said yes, that's him, and asked if I was sure you'd moved away. I gave her a really good performance, moaned about how your removal guys had blocked access to my parking spot with their truck and how inconsiderate that was.'

He laughed out loud. 'Marvellous! What reason did she give for not calling up on the entry phone? Did you ask?'

'She said you'd invited her for lunch, she told me that right at the start, and that you weren't answering the door phone. I suppose she hadn't tried the door phone in case you checked on the camera and wouldn't let her in. So, at the end, I gave her a hard time and said why would you have invited her without saying you'd sold your apartment and moved, and why didn't she just use her phone and call you. And I said it seemed very suspicious to me and I didn't think she knew you at all, so she left in a hurry. Did you have an affair with her?'

'God no, I know hardly anything about her. I've only met her once, at drinks after a talk I gave at an investment firm a few months ago, and then she got my phone number from somewhere, and she started pestering me until I blocked her. I've told her I'm not interested. I asked someone about her the first time she messaged me, and they said she's a bit crazy and to stay well away from her, so after a few messages I blocked her.'

Saskia hesitated for a long time about whether she should ask Orson if he wanted to go out for dinner one night or if it would be best to leave it. The way she felt about him was confusing and hard to define. She knew that the connection she had felt when she sat in his hospital room day after day was a one-sided feeling, one that he had no active part in and was only vaguely aware of by looking back to what his hearing had picked up now and then.

She briefly considered asking Ross what he thought, but it would require too much explaining to set the scene and make him understand her quandary, and he would disapprove of her crazy decision to pretend to be Orson's next of kin. And a moment's thought told her that his thoughts about how to carry on this new whatever-it-was, friendship or relationship, would not be helpful. She was reasonably sure he's just tell her to go for it, and if it didn't work just end it, but that wasn't an option for her at this point in time. I'll tell him later, she thought, when I've got it sorted out in my mind. Her grandmother would have been more useful, she had a surprisingly unconventional attitude to relationships, and she had been a very perceptive woman, but she was no longer around to ask for advice.

The feeling of connection that had built in her mind and her heart while she watched over Orson and worried about him was strong and felt real. Now that she had got to know him a little in what she thought of as the real world, she was fully aware that although the two components of her feelings for him added up to something that felt was very significant, it was also based in part on an illusion and a one-sided thing. He did seem to feel very affectionate towards her, but what kind of affectionate? Was he just fond of her, like a good friend would be, or did those hugs and the way he kissed the palm of her hand mean something more? She couldn't decide, and the ambiguity drove her crazy with frustration. Was he waiting for her to make some sign, or should she just hold back and wait?

What if she thought it was love and it wasn't based on enough reality to last? Would it break her heart to find that it crumbled after a while? Yes, she thought, it probably would break her heart because she already knew he was different from any man she had ever met, in a way she couldn't put her finger on. She had never before felt that someone was so linked to her that if they were hurt or unhappy she would know without even looking at them. That she would drop everything and go to their aid without a thought for her own needs.

Look at the way I never even considered my own life when he was in the hospital, she told herself. I cancelled everything I had planned, only spent nights here in my own home and never thought of leaving him for a moment longer than I had to. I felt so strongly that I must make the best effort I could to make sure he was comforted and felt safe - it wasn't a considered act, it was more like a force of nature, and I just had to do it.

And then she knew the person to discuss this with. Not one of her woman friends who would require lots of explanations to even begin to understand how it had played out. They would put too much emotional emphasis into their responses and want to understand what had prompted her to do what she did and ask too many questions, but they'd never fully get it. There would be too much talking and emoting, and it would drive her mad and achieve nothing. There was only one person who might be able to help her sort it out. She called Henry and asked if he had a little bit of time without clients when she could come in for a chat.

'Come right now, if you can,' he said. 'I've got

nearly an hour free right now - someone cancelled a long appointment. Is something wrong? You sound a bit worked up.'

'I'll explain when I see you, I'll be there in ten minutes max,' she said and started wondering how she would explain it to him, even as she put the phone down. How could she put it so he would understand her dilemma without making it confusing? For God's sake, it's confusing me, she thought as she walked to Henry's, so how can I make it clear to someone else? Perhaps this was a stupid idea, but for some reason I feel he's my only hope.

But once she and Henry sat in the barber's chairs swung towards each other it became simple. Saskia outlined her conflicting thoughts as briefly as she could, the way she had defined things in her mind on the way there, and Henry nodded.

'Of course - I get it,' he said. 'You think it's like you have two deep layers of connection firmly fixed in your mind – or in your heart, I suppose. One layer is what you developed as you sat there in his room and the other is what's developed since you've known him for real, so to speak. And you worry that he's only got one layer, much thinner, or maybe only a half. So, it's unbalanced? Is that it? And you think it might never go any further, build into something lasting?'

'Oh, Henry,' said Saskia gratefully. 'You are such a good friend! You've just put your finger on it, that's exactly it. So, what do you think I should do? Should I risk it? Or stand back and pretend I just think of him as a friend and see what happens?'

'I honestly don't know what you're worrying about,' said Henry with frown creases between his eyebrows, as if he genuinely couldn't see any problems. 'It's not any different from any other love affair, is it? There's always one person in a relationship who loves more strongly than the other, don't you think? Or maybe one who feels more uncertain or exposed than the other, if I can put it that way, or who needs more reassurance. One who is trying harder to please or trying to live up to something, has more doubts. Is this any different?'

Of course, it was no different and that thought slotted into Saskia's head as if it had been whittled into the perfect size and shape to fill the dark hole caused by her conflicted feelings.

'You're a genius, my friend,' she said now and smiled at Henry, who had sat watching her face and waiting for a response while she was thinking. 'You should be a relationship counsellor or some kind of therapist. I feel so relieved now.'

'It's part of the hair dressing training,' said Henry, deadpan and pretend-serious. 'It's one of the hardest modules to pass, but I got an A+.'

They both laughed and talked about other things for a few minutes and then she left, feeling lighter and happier than she had since the day she stood in the hospital corridor and understood she had to leave without seeing Orson.

She was enjoying the story she was constructing, and in a first for her, this one had been nearly fully formed in her mind before she even started. She knew the books in the new genre were only entertainment without any literary merit, but she didn't care. A good story is a good story, she thought, and it will entertain somebody who maybe needs cheering up. Or maybe someone will read it late at night and fall in love with one of the characters. And crime novels had no highbrow value either; the only difference was that her women's fiction would only be bought by women or for women, so half the commercial audience wasn't interested, which would of course influence her publisher.

The call from Matthew came much sooner than she had expected, and she felt a slight frisson of anxiety when she picked her phone up and saw his name. He must have plowed through the books at record speed, so either the verdict was a flat no, or he really liked them. Reading two books so fast had to indicate one extreme or the other, she thought as she let the ringtone continue for a few seconds before she took the call.

'Hi there,' said Matthew, speaking fast and sounding quite abrupt for him. 'I've read both books and I think they're great, I really like them. And so does Joe, by the way, he's read one of them − I hope you don't mind, but he said he thought you'd understand that he's really interested. But I've got to be honest and warn you, because I have serious doubts about what Audrey will think.'

'Oh, I know! She won't like that I've changed genres, and I doubt if she'll accept them as I've written them.' She laughed quietly to herself. 'I can tell you nearly exactly what she'll say about my characters, how she'll ask me to change them, and by the time's she finished with them they won't be mine any longer, they'll be ruined.'

'Exactly!' said Matthew. 'She won't be pleased with the genre change and I don't think she'll like your slightly random characters at all, it's not her sort of fiction. So, she'll probably pressure you to write more crime and make it a condition for rolling the contract over.'

'That's what I thought too,' said Saskia, 'and add to the genre change that this time I would demand some rights re the cover design - I think we'd have a full-blown break-up. Would you suggest them to other publishers?'

'Of course,' said Matthew sounding positive. 'I have a list of possibles in my head to try, but one thing first. Have you thought of marketing them yourself? It might be the only way if you really want so much input into editing and cover design, which I didn't realise until just now. I don't think you can make those demands of a new publisher, after all.'

'I've already considered that. Not that I've looked into the details, but others do it. Do you think I could earn real money doing it myself?'

'You'd be lucky, I think, but maybe if you learnt all the tricks of self-marketing. Or you could hire a book PR firm to market them for you.'

Saskia thought for a moment, absentmindedly reaching up to twist her hair around her finger and finding it too short, which made her laugh. 'I'd quite like to do it myself. I could maybe trade on my track record, don't you think?'

'To some extent, at least, but you wouldn't need an agent if you self-publish.'

There were so many things to consider, and now was not the time to start making choices. First she had to finish the last crime novel and then she would have another three months until the deadline for deciding if the wanted the contract to be renewed. She needed more time to think through all the permutations of how one option would work compared to others.

'I need to think about it, Matthew. It's a big move and I don't know enough about it. We'll park it for now, and I've still got to finish the book Audrey is waiting for, but I'm nearly there now.'

'And don't forget,' said Matthew. 'You'll still have income coming in, probably forever, from books already out there and ebooks and then it's the tv rights etc. I don't think you're going to starve exactly.'

Then Saskia remembered something she had been going to ask him after his and Joe's visit. 'What's Joe's job? You've never told me anything about him. He's such a nice guy.'

'He's a man of many talents - school teacher, kick boxer, good cook and marriage celebrant,' said Matthew. 'I don't know what I ever did to deserve him.'

'So much to think about,' Saskia said out loud when her call with Matthew was over. 'I need to take some time over this. So many balls in the air. I wish I had someone to use as a wall of sensible opinions to bounce all these balls against.'

A couple of days later Saskia picked up her phone, checked the time and texted Orson: *'Would you like to go out for dinner? Any night this week, even tonight if you like.'*

It was four o'clock, so perhaps a bit late to suggest a dinner date, but she wanted to see him so much, and maybe he was free.

His reply came an hour later while she was working on the book about the writer, suddenly inspired again now that Matthew was enthusiastic.

'Of course, tonight is good if it suits you. Could you please come over right now and see what I bought?'

Consumed by curiosity, she quickly called Feriza and booked a table for seven, picked up her keys and went next door to Orson's flat.

'Perhaps we should have a connecting door,' he

said when he let her in. 'Saves all this ringing doorbells and taking keys with us.'

On a mad impulse, Saskia decided to pretend to take this probably light-hearted suggestion seriously, walked ahead of him into his living room and said, 'But what if you have some half-naked woman here on the sofa and I come walking through that as yet non-existent door, wanting to borrow a bottle of wine or whatever?'

Orson gave her a look that was hard to interpret, shook his head and pointed. 'There it is – what do you think?'

Propped up on the low sideboard was a large painting that initially seemed confusing, a nearly totally white painting with a small, black figure walking away from the viewer in the middle-distance and in the far distance the tiny, dark outline of a house with a trace of smoke from the chimney, on a nearly white-on-white horizon. A tiny red rectangle half buried in snow in the extreme foreground might be a letterbox at the start of a very long driveway. Saskia stood as if mesmerised, unable to turn away, her gaze fixed on the tiny figure of that lonely walker.

'Snow,' she said slowly after a moment. 'He's walking through deep snow. Amazing how the snow is painted with just those wide brush strokes, you instantly know it's snow – and his footprints in the snow - I love it, but it makes me sad. All that empty space and he's so alone.'

'Perfect!' said Orson surprisingly. 'Would you like a glass of wine now?'

She turned to look at him, confused by his reaction and unsure about why he had asked her to come, and particularly why he had said 'perfect' in that tone of voice, but instead of asking she just said, 'Yes, please – have you got any white wine, or do you only ever drink red?'

'Of course, I have white wine - I'm only a pretend pirate. Look at me, meticulously shaved three times a week by our friend Henry, hopefully to continue for ever. Would you like champagne perhaps?'

They sat without speaking, side by side on the sofa where they could look across the big room at the painting. Saskia took a sip of champagne and her eyes filled with tears.

'It's you,' she said quietly. She had known it the moment she first saw the paining, and she had hesitated to say it, but now she wanted him to know she understood why he had bought it.

Orson turned his head to meet her eyes. 'Yes, it's me – before I met you. I knew it was about us the moment I saw it through the window at that place down the street from the City Art Gallery.'

She didn't know what to say and a tear overflowed and trickled down her cheek. Orson shifted his glass to his other hand and wiped her cheek with his knuckles. 'Why does it make you sad?'

'I don't know. It's like I'm back out there by the

lift, kneeling in the blood and I can feel it now, that strange sensation that kind of crept up my arms when I held your head so tight, trying to stop the bleeding. That uncanny feeling that I could sense how lonely you were, and I knew I couldn't leave you. I was certain I was right, that you needed me. I didn't cry,' she added hastily. 'Not then, I was too busy praying you wouldn't die and holding on tight. But the painting has brought the feeling back, the loneliness in it feels so real and alive.'

'Saskia, please don't cry,' he said gently. 'I bought it for you. Perhaps it's me walking towards that house in the far distance, perhaps you're in the house?"

She didn't thank him, she just reached out and curled her fingers tight around his and smiled. 'I *am* in that house, Orson, waiting for you and hoping you'll make it through the snow, so I can open the door and pull you into the warmth and hug you.'

They sat there just looking at each other and the silence wasn't an empty space suspended between them, it was like a shared warmth, something to treasure. She had found a person who didn't need to talk or respond all the time. Who could just enjoy thinking and absorbing what had been said and the feeling it generated. I've been looking for him all my life, she thought, and here he is, the man who knows how to share a perfect silence.

'I was hoping you were in that house waiting for

me,' he said finally and now he smiled. 'I didn't know for sure until just now, but I thought you might be.'

Reaching across he took the dangerously tilting champagne flute out of her hand, put it on the table beside his own and pulled her close.

Sometime later, emerging from a long embrace that left her feeling slightly dislocated, as if she had just woken up from a deep sleep, she went back to her flat to get her bag, so they could walk to Feriza for dinner. She knew what she would ask him when they were seated opposite each other, when she could see his face and maybe reach out and take his hand; the questions she had thought she might never be able to ask, but now she knew she could.

Feriza was nearly booked out, but Saskia had managed to talk her way to the end table over by the windows, slightly removed from the bulk of the diners. She had a feeling that a bit of separation from everyone else's chatter and noise might be good for their first meal out together.

'I hope you like Turkish food, and a bit Greek too, I think – or maybe they're sometimes the same thing, like dolma. I love their food, but most of all I love the bathroom.'

Orson shook his head and smiled at the same time. 'So, we're going out for dinner together for the first time and you chose the restaurant based on the bathroom?'

'It's the tiles on the floor,' said Saskia seriously. 'No, I'm not kidding, it's the most gorgeous floor. I fell in love with the floor the first time I saw it and I always go to the bathroom now when I come here, so I can admire the tiles. I'll show you. It's kind of minimalist and creative and decorative all at the same time, if you get what I mean.'

'Perfectly, and very nearly, possibly clear, thank you,' said Orson. 'You come up with words so fast I can't follow you sometimes.'

She got her phone out and scrolled through photos until she found the right one. 'I took this when my dad was staying, and we came here. I wanted to show him the lovely tiles and he refused to come with me to have a quick look.' She laughed at Orson's expression. 'Yes, I know, it sounds mad, but I thought I'd just hold the door open for a moment so he could see, but he declined. Mind you, they might have the same ones in the men's room as well, but I haven't checked.'

She passed to phone to him and waited. 'Mm,' he said after a moment. 'I see what you mean, very nice. I must show you the bathroom next to my bedroom. I had it redone when I bought the apartment because I wanted a walk-in shower. I hope you'll like my tiles too.'

'Ah, well, we can't all like the same things,' she

said and put the phone away, slightly disappointed, just as the waiter arrived to take their orders and then the conversation moved on to other things. It wasn't until they were waiting for dessert that she found the right opportunity to ask the thing she had wondered about for so long.

'Tell me why you're lonely? Have you no friends, no family?'

'God, no - I have quite a lot of family and networks of business acquaintances, but they're spread over the globe. I usually travel to see my family, they rarely come here. But I don't have a lot of friends here, not real friends. I think I'm a bit odd compared to the people you know, people who know how to make new friends, I'm solitary by nature and it doesn't worry me.' He paused for a second. 'Well, it didn't worry me when I was younger. I moved back here from Hong Kong a few years ago when I could see the way things were going there, more and more control from Beijing. And working from home makes it hard to make new friends. I grew up in Timaru, but while I was working first in the England and then in Hong Kong my parents moved back to York in the UK where they'd originally come from.'

'And you siblings followed?'

'Oh, no, they took off in different directions. I've got one brother in Australia, one in Wales and a sister in Romania. We're scattered like confetti across the globe, but I came back to New Zealand, this is where

I want to be, even if I don't know how to make new friends.'

'You're welcome to share mine, I've got a few and they're very nice. And don't forget you have Henry now, too. He's such a lovely guy!'

Orson lifted his glass in a toast, 'He is! Here's to Henry – let's get to know him better.'

She was just about to reply when she saw Bruno approaching from behind Orson's left shoulder and said quietly, 'Oh, for God's sake! *Surely*, he's not going to have the cheek to come and talk to me!'

But he was, brazenly smiling as if nothing unusual had taken place between them. He ignored Orson and stopped beside the table, facing Saskia and swaying slightly. 'Could we have a word in private, Saskia? I think we can sort our problems out.'

He's drunk, thought Saskia, he's *very* drunk and he's acting out some fantasy he has built in his deceitful mind. I never saw him drunk before. Look at him, he can't even focus properly, he's nearly cross-eyed.

'I don't think so - would you please leave,' she said dismissively, but he didn't leave. Instead, he listed sideways, steadied himself with one hand on the edge of their table and said in a slightly slurred voice, 'You look so lovely, come back to me – you know we had a great thing going.'

After listening to this without betraying what he was thinking Orson now got to his feet, took a firm grip on both Bruno's shoulders from behind and moved him physically a couple of steps away from Saskia. 'You should leave now, right now - before I lose my temper! Saskia doesn't want anything to do with you and neither do I.'

'But I just want to ...' started Bruno and Orson interrupted. 'Go and do your wanting somewhere else, you're being offensive.'

'But ...' said Bruno again and Orson swung him around and gave him a little push. 'Buzz off – Saskia's mine, go find your own woman. Or go home to one of your wives.'

Saskia burst out laughing and both men turned to look at her. 'Oh, do fuck off, Bruno,' she exclaimed cheerfully. 'This is the man I want to marry – just go away.'

He started at her for a long moment, and she wondered if he was going to create a scene or start a brawl, then he walked unsteadily away across the room, out the door and disappeared. She turned to Orson. 'He must have spotted me through the window. Well done, Orson! And excuse my language, it just seemed to fit my mood.'

'Are you really?' said Orson and sat down again. 'Did you mean it, marriage? I can't think of anything better.'

'Of course, I meant it! Would I say a thing like that if I didn't mean it?'

He grinned. 'Very likely you would. God knows

what you might come out with, your filter module malfunctions now and then.'

'Orson! I do hope things you stored away in your brain while you lay there like an effigy aren't going to come to the surface and embarrass me for the rest of my life. I said some quite personal things to you in that hospital room.'

'I know, some of them do pop up now and then. Did I dream it, or did you call me a black hole once?'

She studied his face to check he didn't look as if he resented this and tried to explain. 'I felt you were mine, you see, even then, right from the start. First because I felt responsible for you, I didn't want you to be lonely, and then it grew into feeling I was very close to you, connected.' She paused and added thoughtfully, 'Probably aided by various things I won't go into over the dinner table that I helped the nurses do for you.'

His expression now is worth a fortune, she thought as she watched him take this in, it's hilarious. Suspicion and apprehension and laughter all at once. That was a great thing to throw at him, the best one so far.

'Intimate things?'

'Oh, heavens no, don't panic! They always told me to get out of the room for those, I'm just teasing you. But I did help with little things, like I'd hold your tubes and things out of the way when they turned you early in evenings – and I washed your face and brushed your hair, I did that every morning when I arrived.'

'Unbelievable,' said Orson. 'Crashing to the floor outside your flat was the best thing I ever did.'

Stepping out of the lift on level three, Orson said calmly, 'Your place or mine?'

'Oh, yours of course. You've got champagne in the fridge – I don't,' said Saskia on a choke of laughter, feeling as if she was in one of her new women's fiction novels. One where two people finally find each other and something or other eventuates, hopefully. I might have to write this into a book, she thought, slightly disguised, but it's turned into such a good story now.

'Where's your bathroom? I can't have anything more to drink if I don't pee first.'

She followed his pointed gesture but didn't see him standing there waiting until he heard her scream of delight, when he smiled to himself and opened the fridge to get the champagne out.

'Those tiles!' she said when she returned and took the glass he handed her. 'You have those same tiles, and you didn't say a thing in the restaurant. You're very good at this stealth stuff, aren't you?'

'Stealth? No way! I was keeping it as a surprise because I thought it would be worth hearing your reaction when you discovered, as it was.'

Saskia looked first at the glass in her hand and then at Orson, put the glass down and said, 'Let's go to bed.'

He put his own glass beside hers. 'Turn around, please.' From behind he pulled her top over her head very slowly, reached around and equally slowly unzipped her jeans and slid them down. His hands dropped and she stepped out of her shoes and jeans without saying anything. She felt his fingers warm against her skin as he unclipped her bra and let it fall, then his hands on her shoulders turning her around.

'It's like unwrapping a present,' he said and ran his hand over her body. 'The present that's been on my wish list all my life, I just didn't realise exactly what it was I wished for.'

'It's not a present,' said Saskia, standing still, letting his hands roam over her skin, every nerve tingling. 'It's a future. Our future.'

Much later, propped up with her forearms on his chest, she silently studied his face and he said, 'That's a very intense scrutiny, darling. Something wrong with my face? Stubble growing too fast?'

'Oh no, but I was just remembering something I told my dad when we were talking about my notebooks full of thoughts and words and ideas. I told him about a sentence I wrote in my current notebook just recently, but I haven't used it yet, a thing I really liked – a bit ridiculous but funny too.'

'And it was?'

She smiled fondly at his slightly worried look and ran her forefinger lightly over his face as she spoke. 'When I sat in that hospital room I used to look at your face and try to imagine how it would change if you suddenly woke up and opened your eyes and looked at me. This is the sentence I had written in my notebook for future use - before your accident, just by coincidence, but now it feels like fate was telling me something.'

She used her quoting voice: 'Her gaze skated smoothly over the planes of his face like a ballerina on ice, did a pirouette on his forehead and came to rest on his eyes.'

Orson closed his eyes and didn't reply for a few moments, then he said quietly, 'Saskia, you're the best thing that's ever happened to me. It's hard to believe you're real and part of my life. How about we forget about that door in the wall between the flats and you just move in here?'

'But what would I do with my flat? I suppose I could let it if subletting is allowed in the purchase contract.'

'You have lots of options – keep it as a writing studio or sell it? Or sublet it, as you say. Or we make that door in the wall and have a vast flat with more rooms than we can possibly use, about six bedrooms and three balconies for your various balcony activities.'

'And now I'm going to have to tell all my friends

about this, or some of it. But how much do I tell them? I could make it sound a bit less crazy, I suppose, if I leave out the very worst parts of what I did and said, all the lies I told the ambulance crew and at the hospital.'

Orson turned the bedside light off. 'Let's talk about it in the morning, but I think they story is bound to get out now that both Matthew and Joe have heard it, don't you? Maybe an edited version, just leave out the form you signed in ED.'

'Oh, no! I never thought of that when I invited Joe up – Matthew would have kept it to himself, but Joe? Who knows?'

'Don't worry about it now – we'll find some kind of solution,' said Orson. 'Lie down and we'll see if I can think of something to distract you,'

Two days later Orson texted, which was the way they now communicated before seeing each other to make sure the other person wasn't deep in work: *I think I've solved the problem.*

And Saskia replied half an hour later: *The problem about changing genres or what we tell people?*

What we tell people. Come over any time you're not writing. I'm done for today.

'So, what's the answer?' asked Saskia minutes later sitting on a stool at Orson's breakfast counter, after curiosity got the better of her.

'Henry and I came up with the perfect answer. I went for a shave this morning and we were talking about our little problem, and how you feel embarrassed about people finding out how creative and smart you were, pretending to by my cousin. Which neither of us really get, the embarrassment, I mean. We think you're amazing. Why are you looking at me like that?'

'You discussed me with Henry?' Saskia couldn't help feeling a bit hurt because she hadn't realised that Orson and Henry had that kind of friendship. But a second later she was laughing. 'Oh, I'm sorry! Why shouldn't you? I discussed you with Henry more than once. What did you come up with?'

Orson put a cup of something pink and steaming in front of her and said in a reasonable tone of voice, 'Well, the guy shaves me three or four times a week. Of course, we talk about everything. He tells me things about himself and his life, and I tell him things and it goes from there. Being shaved is a very intimate thing. *Now* why are you looking at me like that?'

'What's this pink stuff?'

'God, you're so suspicious today! It's blood orange tea, Henry put me on to it. It's delicious. Anyway, Henry and I think we should have a reveal party.'

'Like American's do? That silly thing when they get their friends together to tell them the sex of their unborn child? Orson, you're not pregnant, are you?'

Orson hauled one of the stools around to the kitchen side and sat down. 'We invite everyone we know between us – those who matter most – and we make it a bit mysterious. As far as we know only Matthew and Joe, Henry and us two even know that we know each other. And Bruno, but I don't count him. Henry thought we would send a text to say we're having a party, from each of us to our friends, as if it's not a couple thing. And we say it's a confession or surprise party or something. We'll have it here because this place is so big. And then we make a production of it.'

Saskia was silent for so long that Orson began to look worried. She stared at his fridge with a vacant look on her face, and he just sat still and watched her, until after a long pause her attention switched back to him.

'Right! I know exactly how we do that. We'll have to invite Ross – he'd be so upset if he wasn't included.'

'Did I tell you I met him?'

'Did you? When he was here this year?'

'We had a short but interesting conversation in the lift one evening. I'd been to the supermarket, and he had been for a walk along the quay. I only know he's your dad because he went into your flat. I had no idea what his name was, or yours for that matter. Nice guy!'

'OK,' said Saskia. 'Please give me a coffee, I don't like this pink tea at all. And let's get Henry over for a planning session, seeing he's totally enmeshed in our lives now. And he's very clever and lovely. I'll invite him for dinner tonight.'

'I think we've cracked it,' said Henry a few hours later, after a sightly circular discussion about the party, coming up with ideas, discarding them and then reviving them again. 'We'll just have to make sure you two don't say too much. We don't want Saskia to be accused of fraud.' He laughed at Saskia's expression. 'Don't panic, I'm kidding! I checked up on this. They could have given him blood or cut him open anyway, even if you hadn't said you're his cousin and signed that form. They've got to if people are unconscious, don't they? So, it makes no difference at all.'

'I'd still rather not go into details — let's just say I told them I was Orson's cousin and leave out the form I signed.' She thought for a moment and added, 'But I'm happy to confess all the rest. There might be few things that Orson doesn't know even now.'

'You can take that wicked look off your face,' said Orson and got up. 'I'm beginning to get the hang of how you work, you know. Your evil tactics to make me blush. Anyone want some more wine?'

Saskia put her hand over her glass. 'I'll wait till we eat. You're not driving, are you, Henry?'

'Driving? Are you mad? You know where I live — it takes five minutes to walk.'

She stared at him. 'Do you live at the salon?'

'Upstairs,' he said and held out his glass. 'I live in a little flat upstairs, well, a two-level flat. You know how narrow that building is, just a room and staircase wide and two rooms deep. I bought it about ten years ago when I inherited quite a lot of money from my last surviving grandparent. So, I've got the salon and the storeroom on ground level, then my kitchen cum living room above that, and then my lovely big bedroom and bathroom at the top. No rent to pay and I don't have to commute to work.'

'I'd love to see it,' said Orson. 'But how does the cat get out, or is it a totally indoor cat? Are you serious about the roof terrace? It would be perfect for the cat.'

Saskia couldn't believe she hadn't known any of this; she didn't even know Henry had a cat. She felt intensely guilty that she had never found out anything about her friend Henry, whom she had trusted with her innermost feelings. The man who had talked her through all her doubts by being so sensible, whom she trusted completely.

She got up and walked around the back of his chair and gave him a hug from behind, kissed his cheek and said, 'I'm sorry, Henry! You've been such a good friend to me, and you've listened to my worries and doubts, and you've made me prettier than I've ever been before – and I didn't ask you a single thing about yourself. So selfish!'

His tattooed hand reached up and patted her arm that was still wound around his neck. 'Don't you worry about that! You were worried about Orson, and then you worried about what you had done, and then you worried again about what it all meant. You didn't have time for much else.'

'That's very generous of you, it really is, and I

don't know that I deserve it. So, here's a genuine question about your private life, one I've been dying to ask. Do you have a woman in your life or are you just a loner like Orson.'

'Very like Orson,' said Henry and laughed. 'Aside from the tattoos. I was married once, and it was a total disaster. The biggest mismatch you've ever seen, based on lust and liking reggae and red wine and not much else, so I got out really fast.'

As soon as Saskia got her father's reply that he could come the weekend after next, she and Orson sat down to compose the text message they would send to their respective friends. After two cups of coffee and many failed attempts they agreed on a version very like the first one they had come up with.

'Typical,' said Orson. 'Go with your instincts, they say, and look at us. We cobbled that first one together so fast and we didn't over-think it, and then we spent the next forty minutes going round in circles trying to improve it - and we're back to where we started more or less. Just like when we discussed what form the party would take.'

A Double Surprise Party with food and wine on Saturday 21ˢᵗ starting at 6.30 (fairly promptly please). RSVP (for catering purposes).

. . .

'Do you think anyone's ever sent a text before with two sets of brackets?' asked Orson when they had finalised it. 'And do you know any caterers? I wouldn't have a clue.'

'Neither do I, and it's no point asking Marian, who's the authority on all things to do with food and entertaining, because she does her own catering even when it's on a huge scale. We'll do a search on the internet. But with thirty-one or was it thirty-two? – we must have food that's easy to eat standing up, don't we?'

Within a very short time after the text invitations went out Saskia was pelted with questions from her friends.

'Bet they're making a film of one of your books!' texted Marian. 'And what's the second surprise?'

'Another Netflix series coming up?' asked Lizzie. 'Let me guess, it's the first and second books in this lot you're writing now. And then another surprise? I can't imagine.'

'I can guess both, so no surprises for me,' said Matthew when he called. 'I imagine this means that you're inviting lots of people? How many can you fit into your living room? And are you inviting Audrey?'

'I don't know,' said Saskia slowly. 'She wasn't on the guest list, but maybe I should. I've known her for years and years after all. But listen, she doesn't even know about the women's fiction books yet, so inviting her would mean I couldn't talk about the change and that would leave us with only one surprise.'

'Hm,' said Matthew. 'Let me think for a moment … maybe I could put those first two women's books in front of her before the party - but no, I don't think so. Leave her out and then you can talk freely about the new books.'

By the beginning of the week after the invitations went out, Saskia had finished the third crime novel in her current series, the one she thought of as her last. After reading through it twice, once on her laptop in "focus" mode and once on her Kindle, she sent it to Audrey with a short message, saying that she would be ready to make any changes they wanted at any time. She deliberately didn't comment on the suggested covers that she had received a few weeks ago. She would rather wait and see what Audrey said about the book, which had an ending she would not have expected; one that might need a completely new cover.

'Saskia, hi!' said Audrey three days later, calling very early in the morning.

'Hi!' said Saskia cheerfully where she sat at the breakfast counter in Orson's kitchen eating crumpets with raspberry jam. 'You've started work very early today, even for you! How are you?'

She flicked her finger over the speaker button and smiled at Orson, who had never met Audrey and might enjoy listening to this.

'I love the book, I really do – but the ending? You must re-work the ending. If this is still supposed to be the final book in this series we can't have a cliff-hanger ending, people hate them. Or are you thinking of a fourth?'

Saskia put her coffee mug down and said, 'It's not a cliff-hanger ending, Audrey, it's a crane-hanger ending. I thought letting the secondary hero die falling from the crane and leaving the real hero dangling was quite a new twist on endings. And no, I'm definitely not writing a fourth one. This is what we agreed on, three books in this series, so that's it.'

'Why are there so many cranes in this book?' asked Audrey. 'I know a lot of it takes place at the container wharf, but we don't even have a crane or a shipping container or anything like it on those cover suggestions I sent you.'

'I know, but I think I remember you saying it didn't matter, the suggested covers kind of fitted with the first two and would look great lined up together?'

A hint of irritation had crept into Audrey's voice. 'I did say that, but that was before I'd read the book. I think we'll have to re-think the cover.'

'Oh, I think so too.' Saskia smiled at Orson and pointed at the toaster where two more crumpets had popped up. 'But as I said at the time, it did seem very early to think of covers before you'd even read the book. Never mind, it's up to you. But I like the ending, I really do.'

'No, you must change it,' said Audrey decisively. 'Change them around. Either the real hero falls and dies, or falls and survives, but we can't leave him hanging from a crane. Let the other guy dangle forever by one hand from that damn crane.'

'OK,' said Saskia and pointed at the raspberry jam. 'I'll swap them around. No problem.' She watched Orson spread butter and raspberry jam on it and said casually, 'Is that the only major change you want?'

Now Audrey's voice sounded nearly petulant. 'Is that all? No objections? I thought you'd fight tooth and nail to keep the ending the way you wrote it.'

'No, it's fine, I don't really mind,' said Saskia airily and bit a tiny bit off her slice of crumpet, met Orson's eyes and tried not to laugh. 'Why don't you send the whole thing back? I'm sure it's full of comment bubbles as usual and I'll fix them for you and send it back in a couple of days.'

'Wow!' said Orson when she ended the call. 'She wasn't expecting that, was she? I presume you usually battle it out. And she wasn't happy about those covers.'

'I know! Wasn't that fun? In the past I've always stuck to my guns about major changes she's suggested, things that really change the story – or a character. So, she's a bit confused now at how easy a victory this thing about the ending was.'

He looked closely at her, then he smiled. 'Aha – I get it now. You're truly wicked sometimes.'

Saskia pointed her nearly eaten crumpet at him and laughed. 'You're getting very good at this. I don't think anyone's ever been able to read me like you do. But wasn't it fun? The real ending, which is very like what she described, is already written. I could email it to her now, but that would spoil the fun.'

She noticed the doubtful look he gave her. 'I'm not being nasty. I only did this because I've made up my mind to move on and not renew the contract. Just a final little game I thought I'd play with her to make up for all the times over the last twelve years I've had to give way to her demands. I'm leaving them, this is the final book of mine they publish.'

'Seriously? Don't you think they'd like to publish the new books?'

'It came to me in the shower yesterday, that even if they said they'd publish my new books and agreed to some new rules, there would always be that history, the kind of ingrained habit of wanting me to change things that matter to me, change how I feel it should be,' said Saskia, intent on making Orson understand what motivated her. 'And it's so frustrating and agonising to have someone else tamper with what my imagination has created. They'll say, "I don't like this" and "I think you could improve on that" as if they were better writers than I am. Improving structure and sometimes the actual plot, yes – they're *very* good at that, but characters, no, absolutely not. Let's face it, they're not authors, are they? From now on I'll be able to do things exactly the way I want.'

Orson chuckled. 'Do you think she'll work it out? I mean, that you were playing games with her about the ending.'

'I don't think so. When I terminate the contract instead of rolling it over she'll just think I couldn't be bothered arguing this final time. But listen, we must confirm the food with the caterers today. I've been through their suggestions and tried to apply Marian's common sense to it.'

She delved into the folder she had left on the counter the previous evening and pulled out two sheets of paper. 'This is what they sent after I asked them to consider that a lot of our guests will eat standing up or sitting with plates on their knees, and I asked them to suggest things that could be carried around on trays instead - for people to just take one and eat it on the spot. You can feed people a whole meal like that quite easily. We'll need a waiter or two or someone's kids to run around with trays – refill them and all that. You can see what I've crossed out. There are only two things I won't have deleted - salmon roulade and feta and spinach pastry roll. They're my two favourite things.'

'OK, fine with me,' said Orson. 'Now come with

me.' He walked ahead of her down the wide hallway to the bedrooms. 'This is a room you could have for a writing room if you sublet your apartment.'

The room was empty and had the same view as her living room and she realised she hadn't even registered there was a room between the living room and the master bedroom.

'I never noticed,' she said. 'How funny, every time we've gone to your bedroom I've walked past this closed door and never thought of what it was. Blinded by lust, probably. Why is it empty?'

Orson shook his head and gave her that funny look he aimed at her sometimes, a mock "are you serious?" look that she particularly enjoyed.

'This is designated as a study on the floorplan, believe it or not. I don't need it as a guest room, I've got two of those already and nobody to put in them. Nobody's come to stay since I moved back here because I always go and see them, I do a round trip and visit everyone.'

'It's lovely, I could move my armchairs and the coffee table in here and my little desk too, plenty of space – like a little writer's living room.'

'Or you could turn this into a guest room and have one of the other rooms as your writing room. I imagine you want a separate room rather than work in the living room like I do.'

I don't know,' said Saskia slowly. I've never thought of living with anyone before, so I don't know how it would work. I'm not sure how important the total silence is because that's what I've always had. Do you always sit at the dining table and work?'

'All I need is a notepad and my laptop, I can work anywhere. Sometimes I stand up and have the laptop on the breakfast counter – it's the perfect height. And you worked in my room at the hospital, but I suppose I didn't make a lot of noise. You can organise things any way you like or change to another room later on – or work at the dining table. So long as you're happy I don't care how you rearrange things.'

'And?' asked Saskia who knew now how to detect the unspoken thought he often held back for a while. 'Another idea?'

'Perhaps you could stop talking about the master bedroom as mine and call it ours, or just the bedroom? I don't care if you live here all the time or move between your place and mine, that bedroom is ours.'

'Orson, you're such a lovely bear,' said Saskia and reached up to kiss him. 'I'm very lucky to have you.'

Chapter 29

The day of the party turned into non-stop activity that left no time for worrying about the evening ahead, and no time to start discussing Saskia's sudden doubts about the wisdom of what they were doing. It's too late, she told herself as she had a careful shower so as not to ruin the wonderful blow-dry job Henry had done for her yesterday, with enough product in it to make it last. I can't start changing things now, we've got this scripted and I'll just have to endure it.

Saskia met Ross's flight from Sydney at half past eleven, after she and Orson had spent a couple of hours moving furniture and then cleared his kitchen benches to a state of total emptiness for the caterers, who were due to arrive at five that afternoon. She knew Ross could easily have got himself into town, but ever since he moved to Sydney she had always met him at the airport. She had been careful to reveal a minimum of detail about Orson to Ross, and though this had been easy over the phone, it was much harder when he sat beside her in the car. By the time they parked in the underground carpark she was frustrated by the effort it took to not tell him too much but still satisfy his curiosity.

'Dad, please listen!' she said as they walked to the lift. 'I know you like to have your facts straight, and I do understand you don't like all this evasiveness, but if you could just hold on until tonight I'd be very grateful. I've always told you things before, but this time you have to wait along with everyone else. Apart from a couple of people, who unavoidably found out, our guests tonight have no idea Orson and I even know each other. Even my best woman friends don't know a thing. Let's just say that I kind of meddled in Orson's life before we knew each other, with the best of intentions, of course – and it got a bit complicated. You'll get the details tonight at the party, as I said.'

They entered Saskia's apartment and found that Orson had croissants, ham and lettuce set out on the table with newly made coffee and to Saskia's surprise, a thermos, which made her laugh.

'Dad,' she said. 'This is Orson, the man I've been waiting for all my life, who actually turned out to live next door.' She turned to Orson. 'A thermos! I haven't seen one of those since I was on a dig with dad years ago, but that one was full of cold water. Coffee in this one, I hope.'

'Hi,' said Ross calmly and reached out to shake Orson's hand. 'We've met before - we had a chat in the lift a few months ago. I gather your life's been taken over by Saskia. She sometimes blurs the lines between her stories and real life, and then anything can happen.'

'Hi Ross, nice to see you again,' said Orson equally calmly. 'I'm familiar with the blurred lines, and I don't mind at all. I'm very happy to be part of her world, real or imagined. I've never met anyone so interesting in my life before. But I think you'll be surprised when you hear the full story tonight. And any bits we decide to leave out then, we'll tell you later, the very personal ones.'

He turned to Saskia and gave her that look of his. 'Of course, it's coffee in the thermos. God knows how much we're going to need before tonight, because we're going to be busy - I've just had another idea about how we can move a few things around at my place, so it will work even better tonight.'

At quarter past six Saskia's nerves were jangling with apprehension. She checked that her front door was locked and tied the balloon to the doorhandle, then she stuck her bright pink sign on with Blu-tack and stood back to admire it: *Change of venue, the party is now next door* with a big arrow pointing left to Orson's front door, which was going to be left open.

By seven their guests had arrived, been given drinks and introduced to whichever of the hosts they didn't already know, the caterers were busy circulating trays of finger food, and the noise level was rising rapidly. Henry who appointed himself to the role of master of ceremonies, claiming he had always wanted to be in a theatre production, picked up a little brass bell Saskia had dug out of her Christmas box. He held it high and rang it until all conversation stopped and the big room was silent, with only distant traffic noise filtering in through the open balcony doors.

'Hi,' he said, standing beside Orson and Saskia. 'I'm Henry. Orson and I have become good friends because I've shaved him with this every couple of days for some weeks now.'

He pulled his cut-throat razor from his pocket and unfolded it, held it up and clicked it shut again. The silence was total now, and people glanced at each other unsure of what to make of this. 'I'm also a friend of Saskia's and I gave her that new hairstyle that makes her even prettier than she was already.'

He took a sip of his wine, cleared his throat and continued, 'This is not the night of two surprises, it's actually the night of many surprises. The first one is that these two are a couple, not just neighbours.'

He held up his hand and silenced the murmur of comments. 'Let's keep all reactions for the really exciting stuff a bit later, please. There's lots more to come. Now, if the wait staff could go around and top up everyone's glass I'll continue while they do that. This story will be told by the three of us taking turns, because we all had a role to play in this story, and some of it needs to be told by the person most concerned – or by the person who was conscious at the time.'

More murmurs in the crowd and once again his hand went up and gradually the room became silent again. As they had agreed when they mapped out how the story telling would work, Saskia started.

'One night when I was sitting up late watching TV I heard a strange beeping sound …' She continued with a vivid description of how she found Orson lying with his head in a puddle of blood, called the ambulance and put pressure on his wound.

'And then,' she said and paused, aware that she was about to irrevocably reveal something deeply personal, nearly too personal. 'As soon as I held his head with both hands I felt something. Like a little stream of consciousness flowing up my arms and I knew without a doubt that he was lonely. And in that moment I also knew I couldn't possibly leave him, I had to stay with him whatever happened next.'

She continued with her rushed change of jeans, the trip to ED and what happened over the next few hours.

'And then,' she said coolly, having recovered her

inner composure, and smiled at Orson who was standing beside her. 'Then I went back to the hospital early the next morning and said I was his cousin, told multiple lies and behaved in a very deceitful manner to get them to let me in, even though it was hours before visiting time. And that wonderful woman over there in the red dress, nurse Wendy, let me in. And from then I spent two weeks in Orson's hospital room from half past eight in the morning until nine or ten at night.'

This time there was no stopping the comments and questions, and it was Orson's turn to take over. He put an arm around Saskia's shoulder sand pulled her close, and Henry pulled the little bell out of his pocket and rang it until the room was silent again.

'So, there I was,' said Orson, 'in a coma with a head fracture and a big, stitched wound in my head, lying in my bed like an effigy, as Saskia says. But I heard some things that went on in that room despite being in a coma, and I do remember some of them - other things Saskia has told me later. How she came in and brushed my hair every morning and wiped my face with cold water. That she sat at a little table in the corner that lovely Wendy had provided and continued to write the book that had a deadline coming up, and how she stopped to talk to me now and then and sang to me, and tried everything she could think of to stimulate me, in case somewhere inside my head I could hear her.'

Saskia smiled at him. 'And he could hear some things, bits of phone conversations, things I said to him and sometimes things I probably shouldn't have said. He tells me he felt my hand on his cheek and how I ran my fingers over his stubble.'

The story continued between the three of them with Henry relating how Saskia came to hire him to shave Orson "because she didn't like him looking like a pirate", and how their friendship evolved, and she let him cut her hair. Saskia described how she suddenly realised she couldn't go back the day after Orson regained consciousness, and Orson told the story of standing by the lift in total darkness on the night of the blackout and suddenly realising who Saskia was when he heard her singing on the stairs. He described how they sat in her living room and drank red wine by candlelight and how connected to her he felt.

'So, there you have it', said Henry when they reached the end. 'Probably the most fascinating love story ever. I've certainly not heard or read anything to unusual and romantic. Someone should write a book about it. Let's have a toast to these two wonderful people.'

Five minutes later, after laughter and congratulations, Henry rang his bell again. 'And now for the final surprise.' He looked around, beckoned someone forward and said, now very serious, 'Let me introduce Joe, who is the husband of Matthew, who in his turn is Saskia's agent. Apart from being a schoolteacher and a kick boxer, Joe is also a registered marriage celebrant, and he's going to marry Saskia and Orson right now, right here, before the party continues.'

They were married in a five-minute ceremony standing just inside the open doors to the balcony without flowers or fuss, with all their friends present and only Orson's family absent. Wendy and Henry signed the forms as witnesses and then the full onslaught started. People crowded around them, hugged and kissed them, and asked a thousand questions. Ross told everyone who would listen that he hadn't had the slightest idea what would happen, and Wendy admitted she had only that day discovered the couple weren't cousins and hadn't known they would make her a wedding witness until she arrived.

The party went on with food constantly circulating, people who had never met or even heard about each other became friends by sharing stories about either Orson or Saskia. Very late and feeling exhausted by strong emotions and endlessly repeating the same answers to the same questions, Saskia found herself corralled into a corner by Marian and Lizzie.

'No!' she said decisively. 'Stop it! We can't talk here, let's go to the other end.'

She led the way down the hallway, through their

bedroom and out onto the balcony where she had recently put a small table and four chairs, so they could sit on whichever balcony was out of the wind.

'Orson never used this balcony,' she said and sat down in one of the chairs with a sigh of relief. 'I bought this stuff the other day, it's nice to have a slightly different view.'

'You are without any doubt the most devious woman in the country,' said Marian. 'All this going on and not a hint to either of us! It's unbelievable - we're your best friends!'

'I know, and I'm sorry I had to keep you in the dark, but it was so strange. The whole thing went from me doing something crazy, and then thinking I must have been insane to do it, to this! And not knowing if Orson felt anything for me other than gratitude. And I was so glad Henry changed my hair, so Orson wouldn't recognise me from that short time he was conscious, but of course, in the end he did discover I lived next door, as you heard. So much doubt and hesitation and trepidation on my side about what he would say or do if he found out it was me.'

'But the staff at the hospital must have told him your name, of course he knew who you were,' said Lizzie. 'He could have found you easily, just Googled you and worked out where you lived.'

'He told me later he was going to do that, he'd looked me up on the publisher's website and checked out details, but they still have the photo of me from before Henry cut my hair, and Orson failed to find an address for me. He had no idea I was living next door, but he was getting up the courage to email the publishers and ask them to forward a message. He had no idea what to make of it, and he didn't know how it started, nothing!'

She looked from one to the other and added. 'If I had told anyone, who was emotionally involved with me about what I'd done, like you two, it would have overwhelmed me. You have no idea about the doubt and the feelings that kept alternating in my mind. The devastating thought that he'd never know that I felt from the very start that I knew him, how much I loved him. I tortured myself over it, and I could see no way forward. Henry was my comfort and my sounding board, he knew it all nearly from the start, of course, and he could look at it from a cooler perspective, and he gave me such good advice, he's so sensible. And now he's our friend.'

Chapter 30

At half past two in the morning, many hours after the caterers had tidied up their things and gone, the last guests congratulated, hugged and kissed their way out the door. Saskia, Ross and Orson stood looking at each other in the disordered living room, exhausted but smiling.

'I think I'll go next door and go straight to bed,' said Ross. 'It's a long time since I was up this late or had such an exciting evening. Who was the guy filming the whole thing?'

'A friend of mine from university,' said Orson. 'He came up from Wellington with his wife for the event, said he'd never heard of me entertaining before, so he had to come. He said he only decided to film it when Henry rang the bell, and he realised it was going to be a performance or announcement of some kind.'

'I didn't even notice anyone filming.' Saskia

yawned. 'I was so concentrated on our story that I didn't see anyone clearly. Was he that guy with the beard you introduced me to, Alex?'

Orson nodded. 'That's him, and his wife was the very skinny woman with an asymmetric haircut and purple streaks. I saw Henry talking to her for quite a while.'

'He was probably giving her hair advice – or else he was offering her counselling.' Saskia laughed and yawned at the same time. 'He's such a multi-talented guy, our Henry.'

When the three of them met Henry, Matthew and Joe for brunch at the Wynyard Pavilion the next day, they had to sit inside to avoid what looked a possible shower of rain.

'Again!' said Saskia and scowled at the clouds. 'Why are we living in this mad city? But they've given us the best table, so I'll shut up about the weather.'

'And what are you doing with your apartment?' asked Matthew when they had ordered. 'Are you going to live in Orson's or are you going to have one each?'

'God no! I've decided to sub-let mine,' said Saskia. 'And then if my new books don't sell, and everything turns to mud, I'll have some money coming in. And by the way, did I remember to tell you I don't want you to show Audrey my women's books?'

'I haven't done anything with them yet, but why not show them to her?' Matthew looked confused. 'Have I missed something here?'

'I've decided I'm tired of being edited by professionals,' said Saskia and nearly laughed at his expression and remembering his suggestions about her last book before it went to the publishers. 'I'm not renewing my contract and I'll market the new books myself. To tell you the truth, I've had enough of trying to justify why my characters are the way they are – it's like an assault on my personality.'

Ross broke in and changed the subject. 'Can I live in your flat? If you haven't already promised it to someone else, of course.'

'Are you coming back to live here?' She couldn't believe her ears. He had lived in Sydney for nearly twenty years and had half of his original family there. 'Why? Are you leaving the university?'

'I've got a year's sabbatical to write a book, so it seemed nice to do it from here.'

Matthew grinned at him and said, 'So I lose one author and maybe I'll gain another? What's the book about?'

Ross said mock seriously, 'I'm going to call it "Modern methodological tools for dating archaeological artefacts" – for short. The long title takes up five lines.'

'Not my thing, sorry! Try the University of Chicago Press,' said Matthew dead-pan as usual.

'They publish a lot of things like that, books with difficult titles that take up the whole cover.'

'He knows everything,' said Saskia in a loud whisper to Ross. 'Or he might be making it up.' Aloud she added, 'You're welcome to the flat for your sabbatical.'

Henry changed the subject just as a waiter appeared with their plates, looked at Joe and said, 'If I decide to get married again, would you marry me?'

'Sorry, I can't - I'm already married to Matthew. But if you mean would I perform the ceremony, yes, of course.'

Now they all stared at Henry, who calmly picked up his knife and fork as if nothing unusual had happened and said nothing more.

Finally, Orson broke the silence. 'I hope you didn't fall in love with Alex's wife last night! I saw you two chatting for quite a while in a corner.'

'God no, she's too skinny for me. I like women with a bit of bulk, something to grab hold of on a cold night. But I'm very taken with nurse Wendy, gorgeous woman - and funny.'

'Had you two got acquainted before the party – I mean at the hospital?' Saskia felt slightly confused. 'And if you had, I hope you hadn't let anything out of the bag prior to last night.'

'Of course not, I hadn't told her anything about you! What do you take me for? But we talked now and then at the hospital, and we've had coffee a couple of times. I really like her.'

'Maybe it's catching – marriage, I mean,' said Ross. 'Like yawns.'

Late that evening, after a makeshift dinner of party left-overs, when Ross had returned to Saskia's flat, Orson said, 'Do you know what the best thing today was?'

'Lunch?' suggested Saskia. 'Or maybe when Henry asked Joe to marry him?'

'No, it was when we arrived and I said to the waitress that my wife had booked it, but I didn't know what name she had used. It was the first time I'd said, "my wife". Such a nice feeling.'

'Oh, Orson,' said Saskia. 'You *are* such a lovely bear.'

Letters from the Past

Letters from the Past is a series of stand-alone novels where a letter from or about the past reveals something that changes a woman's perceptions of herself or of her family, and that affects her outlook on life.

These books are such fun to write, and I am always working on the next title in this series. I hope you will enjoy reading them as much as I enjoy writing them!

Tina

Having had nobody in her life since her husband died, Lara unexpectedly finds herself involved with three men. One is planning to use her, one she plans to use for her own ends, and one becomes a "friend-with-benefits" with surprising results. Sometimes a quiet schoolteacher is not all she seems at first glance.

Callista experiences an event of apparent ESP at the Okehampton Castle ruins and becomes a media sensation, but the effect it has on her life is dramatic. How do two people, one calm. one seriously claustrophobic, who feel they are poles apart, cope for an hour and a half in total darkness in a stalled lift? And can they handle the consequences?

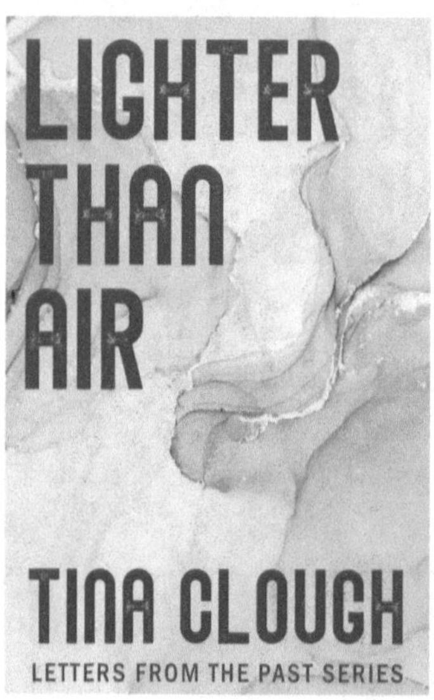

Sofia's life is in turmoil: a difficult diva mother, a letter with a confession about a family killing and having to accept help from a man she loathes when she is injured. Can reluctant attraction turn into love?

Who is the stranger living in the empty house Miranda inherited from her grandmother? Why is he living like a secretive recluse in someone else's house? Reckless Miranda decides to confront him, and what she discovers prompts her to set out on a fearless quest to bring justice to a man who has given up hope. But is the gamble too great or a risk worth taking?

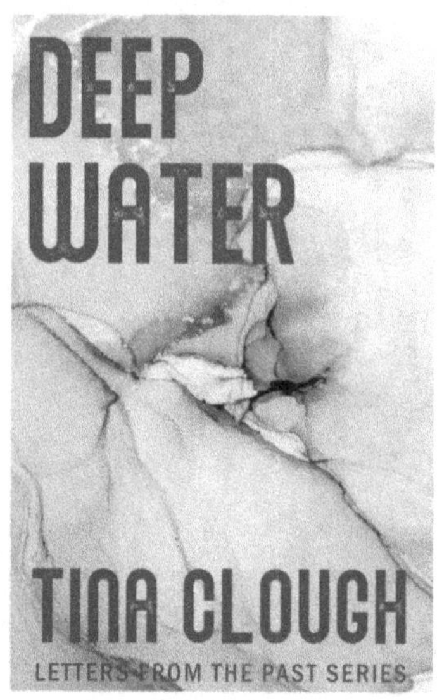

When Emma finds an old letter in a library book she is instantly intrigued, but by researching the origin of the letter she unwittingly opens the door to danger and becomes the target for threats and harassment. Nearly desperate, she takes a leap of blind faith into the unknown and accepts an offer of help from a stranger - but can she trust him?

Jamie, an ardent protester against the gigantic Vista Resort development and Leo Masters, the high-powered developer, seem unlikely to ever agree on anything. But unexpected coincidences and chance brings them together in a fragile state of mutual respect. Will courage and kindness resolve the situation, or do they need help?

After a bizarre accident with ESP overtones, the media haunt Arapera. But can she trust an offer of help from a man she has only met once? Or will she regret it for the rest of her life if she doesn't take the chance? Sometimes life is a knife-edge balance between staying safe and taking risks, and there is no way of predicting if the gamble is worth it.

When crime-writer Saskia finds an unconscious stranger, she has a strange and strong emotional connection. Pretending to be his cousin and with no thought for the consequences, she spends weeks at his hospital bedside. But what will happen when he wakes and discovers she has invaded his life, breached his privacy and made crucial decisions on his behalf?

THE GIRL WHO LIVED TWICE

What would you do if you woke up one morning and found that time had rewound exactly a year? Would you revisit your past mistakes and try to do better? Would you try to get revenge on those who had wronged you? Or would you use what you knew to get rich? When Mia finds herself in her own past, she must decide how best to use her pre-knowledge of one year's worth of events and personal issues.

RUNNING TOWARDS DANGER

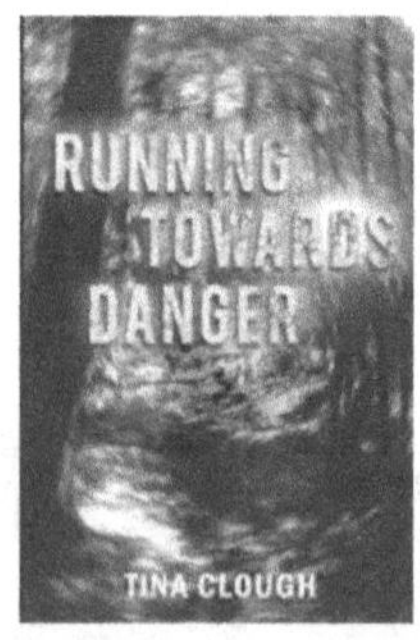

When Karen's flat-mate Nick is gunned down in front of her in the street her life is turned upside-down. Everything she thought she knew about him turns out to be a lie. She becomes a suspect in the police investigation and drug bosses think she knows where Nick has hidden a large sum of money. When her life is threatened, she decides to leave town and disappear.

Karen becomes Cara and creates an anonymous existence, severs all links to her past and adopts a cash-based way of life that leaves no electronic traces. But despite her careful planning danger still stalks her and she is forced to make dramatic choices in the face of threats and brutal violence.

Can she trust the man she is attracted to, or has he been sent by the killers to gain her confidence and find the money they believe she has?

THE CHINESE PROVERB

Book 1 - Hunter Grant Series

Army veteran Hunter Grant thought he had left war behind in Afghanistan – a conflict that left him with physical and psychological scars.

But finding an unconscious girl in the Northland bush and gradually untangling her story involves him in warfare of a different kind in his own country.

Hunter sets out to find and punish the man Dao calls Master, but he soon finds there is more to this story than enslavement. Before long he himself is being hunted by the overlord of a drug empire whose sole objective is to kill Dao because she knows too much.

Protecting her and waging war while trying to keep the police from stifling his enterprise takes all Hunter's ingenuity and determination and puts him in deadly jeopardy.

ONE SINGLE THING

Book 2 - Hunter Grant Series

Journalist Hope Barber disappears two weeks after returning to New Zealand from an assignment in Pakistan, leaving her front door open and her bag and phone inside. The police are tight-lipped about their reluctance to act, and Hunter Grant and Dao agree to help Hope's brother Noah find her. Details about Hope's time in Pakistan gradually emerge but only raise more questions.

Was Hope under surveillance?

Was she linked to terrorists?

And who is the man Hope called 'my stalker'?

FOLDED

Book 3 - Hunter Grant Series

First notes asking for help and folded into tiny origami shapes are found outside a city apartment building, then a physics textbook with tiny writing between the lines and then the woman who found them abruptly resigns and disappears. Are the notes asking for help real or is it a game? Hunter Grant, ex-army and with a pragmatic view of justice, reluctantly agrees to help find the missing woman.

Things get complicated when a high-powered lawyer arrives form the US, and shortly after his meeting with Hunter and Dao, a "cease and desist" letter arrives from the Cayman Islands. Inspector Bakker - a woman, who in Hunter's words "looks as if she would be useful in a brawl, provided she was on your side" - takes instant exception to his involvement and threatens to arrest him for interfering in an investigation.

Dao sets out alone on a dangerous mission, driven by a compulsive need to find out what has happened to the girl who wrote the notes, and Hunter looks death in the face when he decides to risk everything to put an end to the Darknet forces that threaten their lives.

THE SHADOW BROKER

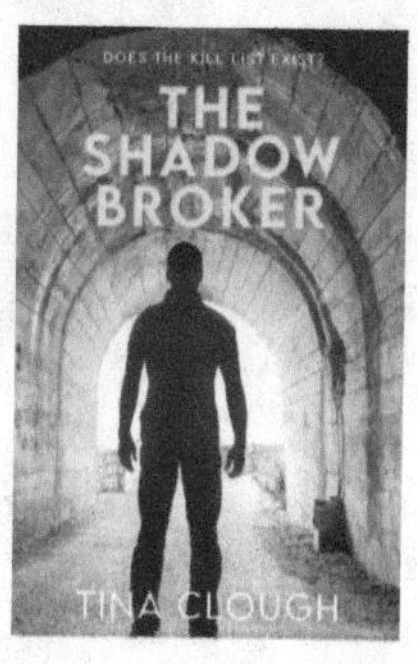

It is 2026 and individual freedoms are severely curtailed, with state surveillance everywhere. State Security has a Watch List, and being on it means that nothing you do or say escapes the authorities, but does the Kill List really exist? And if it does, how would you know if you were on it?

Coded messages on a found burner phone, top-level government corruption and a shadowy mastermind who calls himself The Broker. In this climate of state control, three unlikely friends start quietly looking for connections and set in motion a deadly game of hide and seek that will change their lives forever.

Trying to uncover the truth means risking your life, and nothing is more dangerous than searching for evidence of government corruption.

About the Author

Tina Clough grew up in Sweden and now lives in New Zealand; dividing her time between writing fiction and translating and editing medical research papers.

Between working and writing she looks after an acre of fruit trees, vegetable gardens and roaming hens.

Apart from reading her interests include photography, wine, growing organic vegetables, making jam and kayaking.

https://lightpoolpublishing.com

* 9 7 8 1 9 9 1 1 8 7 1 7 8 *